SO FAR GONE

(A Faith Bold Mystery —Book Five)

BLAKE PIERCE

Blake Pierce

Blake Pierce is the USA Today bestselling author of the RILEY PAGE mystery series, which includes seventeen books. Blake Pierce is also the author of the MACKENZIE WHITE mystery series, comprising fourteen books; of the AVERY BLACK mystery series, comprising six books; of the KERI LOCKE mystery series, comprising five books; of the MAKING OF RILEY PAIGE mystery series, comprising six books; of the KATE WISE mystery series, comprising seven books; of the CHLOE FINE psychological suspense mystery, comprising six books; of the JESSIE HUNT psychological suspense thriller series, comprising twenty-eight books; of the AU PAIR psychological suspense thriller series, comprising three books; of the ZOE PRIME mystery series, comprising six books; of the ADELE SHARP mystery series, comprising sixteen books, of the EUROPEAN VOYAGE cozy mystery series, comprising six books; of the LAURA FROST FBI suspense thriller, comprising eleven books; of the ELLA DARK FBI suspense thriller, comprising fourteen books (and counting); of the A YEAR IN EUROPE cozy mystery series, comprising nine books, of the AVA GOLD mystery series, comprising six books; of the RACHEL GIFT mystery series, comprising ten books (and counting); of the VALERIE LAW mystery series, comprising nine books (and counting); of the PAIGE KING mystery series, comprising eight books (and counting); of the MAY MOORE mystery series, comprising eleven books; of the CORA SHIELDS mystery series, comprising eight books (and counting); of the NICKY LYONS mystery series, comprising eight books (and counting), of the CAMI LARK mystery series, comprising eight books (and counting), of the AMBER YOUNG mystery series, comprising five books (and counting), of the DAISY FORTUNE mystery series, comprising five books (and counting), of the FIONA RED mystery series, comprising five books (and counting), of the FAITH BOLD mystery series, comprising eight books (and counting), of the JULIETTE HART mystery series, comprising five books (and counting), of the MORGAN CROSS mystery series, comprising five books (and counting), and of the new FINN WRIGHT mystery series, comprising five books (and counting).

An avid reader and lifelong fan of the mystery and thriller genres, Blake loves to hear from you, so please feel free to visit www.blakepierceauthor.com to learn more and stay in touch.

ISBN: 978-1-0943-8226-5

BOOKS BY BLAKE PIERCE

FINN WRIGHT MYSTERY SERIES
WHEN YOU'RE MINE (Book #1)
WHEN YOU'RE SAFE (Book #2)
WHEN YOU'RE CLOSE (Book #3)
WHEN YOU'RE SLEEPING (Book #4)
WHEN YOU'RE SANE (Book #5)

MORGAN CROSS MYSTERY SERIES
FOR YOU (Book #1)
FOR RAGE (Book #2)
FOR LUST (Book #3)
FOR WRATH (Book #4)
FOREVER (Book #5)

JULIETTE HART MYSTERY SERIES
NOTHING TO FEAR (Book #1)
NOTHING THERE (Book #2)
NOTHING WATCHING (Book #3)
NOTHING HIDING (Book #4)
NOTHING LEFT (Book #5)

FAITH BOLD MYSTERY SERIES
SO LONG (Book #1)
SO COLD (Book #2)
SO SCARED (Book #3)
SO NORMAL (Book #4)
SO FAR GONE (Book #5)
SO LOST (Book #6)
SO ALONE (Book #7)
SO FORGOTTEN (Book #8)

FIONA RED MYSTERY SERIES
LET HER GO (Book #1)
LET HER BE (Book #2)
LET HER HOPE (Book #3)

LET HER WISH (Book #4)
LET HER LIVE (Book #5)

DAISY FORTUNE MYSTERY SERIES
NEED YOU (Book #1)
CLAIM YOU (Book #2)
CRAVE YOU (Book #3)
CHOOSE YOU (Book #4)
CHASE YOU (Book #5)

AMBER YOUNG MYSTERY SERIES
ABSENT PITY (Book #1)
ABSENT REMORSE (Book #2)
ABSENT FEELING (Book #3)
ABSENT MERCY (Book #4)
ABSENT REASON (Book #5)

CAMI LARK MYSTERY SERIES
JUST ME (Book #1)
JUST OUTSIDE (Book #2)
JUST RIGHT (Book #3)
JUST FORGET (Book #4)
JUST ONCE (Book #5)
JUST HIDE (Book #6)
JUST NOW (Book #7)
JUST HOPE (Book #8)

NICKY LYONS MYSTERY SERIES
ALL MINE (Book #1)
ALL HIS (Book #2)
ALL HE SEES (Book #3)
ALL ALONE (Book #4)
ALL FOR ONE (Book #5)
ALL HE TAKES (Book #6)
ALL FOR ME (Book #7)
ALL IN (Book #8)

CORA SHIELDS MYSTERY SERIES
UNDONE (Book #1)
UNWANTED (Book #2)

UNHINGED (Book #3)
UNSAID (Book #4)
UNGLUED (Book #5)
UNSTABLE (Book #6)
UNKNOWN (Book #7)
UNAWARE (Book #8)

MAY MOORE SUSPENSE THRILLER
NEVER RUN (Book #1)
NEVER TELL (Book #2)
NEVER LIVE (Book #3)
NEVER HIDE (Book #4)
NEVER FORGIVE (Book #5)
NEVER AGAIN (Book #6)
NEVER LOOK BACK (Book #7)
NEVER FORGET (Book #8)
NEVER LET GO (Book #9)
NEVER PRETEND (Book #10)
NEVER HESITATE (Book #11)

PAIGE KING MYSTERY SERIES
THE GIRL HE PINED (Book #1)
THE GIRL HE CHOSE (Book #2)
THE GIRL HE TOOK (Book #3)
THE GIRL HE WISHED (Book #4)
THE GIRL HE CROWNED (Book #5)
THE GIRL HE WATCHED (Book #6)
THE GIRL HE WANTED (Book #7)
THE GIRL HE CLAIMED (Book #8)

VALERIE LAW MYSTERY SERIES
NO MERCY (Book #1)
NO PITY (Book #2)
NO FEAR (Book #3)
NO SLEEP (Book #4)
NO QUARTER (Book #5)
NO CHANCE (Book #6)
NO REFUGE (Book #7)
NO GRACE (Book #8)
NO ESCAPE (Book #9)

RACHEL GIFT MYSTERY SERIES
HER LAST WISH (Book #1)
HER LAST CHANCE (Book #2)
HER LAST HOPE (Book #3)
HER LAST FEAR (Book #4)
HER LAST CHOICE (Book #5)
HER LAST BREATH (Book #6)
HER LAST MISTAKE (Book #7)
HER LAST DESIRE (Book #8)
HER LAST REGRET (Book #9)
HER LAST HOUR (Book #10)

AVA GOLD MYSTERY SERIES
CITY OF PREY (Book #1)
CITY OF FEAR (Book #2)
CITY OF BONES (Book #3)
CITY OF GHOSTS (Book #4)
CITY OF DEATH (Book #5)
CITY OF VICE (Book #6)

A YEAR IN EUROPE
A MURDER IN PARIS (Book #1)
DEATH IN FLORENCE (Book #2)
VENGEANCE IN VIENNA (Book #3)
A FATALITY IN SPAIN (Book #4)

ELLA DARK FBI SUSPENSE THRILLER
GIRL, ALONE (Book #1)
GIRL, TAKEN (Book #2)
GIRL, HUNTED (Book #3)
GIRL, SILENCED (Book #4)
GIRL, VANISHED (Book 5)
GIRL ERASED (Book #6)
GIRL, FORSAKEN (Book #7)
GIRL, TRAPPED (Book #8)
GIRL, EXPENDABLE (Book #9)
GIRL, ESCAPED (Book #10)
GIRL, HIS (Book #11)
GIRL, LURED (Book #12)

GIRL, MISSING (Book #13)
GIRL, UNKNOWN (Book #14)

LAURA FROST FBI SUSPENSE THRILLER
ALREADY GONE (Book #1)
ALREADY SEEN (Book #2)
ALREADY TRAPPED (Book #3)
ALREADY MISSING (Book #4)
ALREADY DEAD (Book #5)
ALREADY TAKEN (Book #6)
ALREADY CHOSEN (Book #7)
ALREADY LOST (Book #8)
ALREADY HIS (Book #9)
ALREADY LURED (Book #10)
ALREADY COLD (Book #11)

EUROPEAN VOYAGE COZY MYSTERY SERIES
MURDER (AND BAKLAVA) (Book #1)
DEATH (AND APPLE STRUDEL) (Book #2)
CRIME (AND LAGER) (Book #3)
MISFORTUNE (AND GOUDA) (Book #4)
CALAMITY (AND A DANISH) (Book #5)
MAYHEM (AND HERRING) (Book #6)

ADELE SHARP MYSTERY SERIES
LEFT TO DIE (Book #1)
LEFT TO RUN (Book #2)
LEFT TO HIDE (Book #3)
LEFT TO KILL (Book #4)
LEFT TO MURDER (Book #5)
LEFT TO ENVY (Book #6)
LEFT TO LAPSE (Book #7)
LEFT TO VANISH (Book #8)
LEFT TO HUNT (Book #9)
LEFT TO FEAR (Book #10)
LEFT TO PREY (Book #11)
LEFT TO LURE (Book #12)
LEFT TO CRAVE (Book #13)
LEFT TO LOATHE (Book #14)
LEFT TO HARM (Book #15)

LEFT TO RUIN (Book #16)

THE AU PAIR SERIES
ALMOST GONE (Book#1)
ALMOST LOST (Book #2)
ALMOST DEAD (Book #3)

ZOE PRIME MYSTERY SERIES
FACE OF DEATH (Book#1)
FACE OF MURDER (Book #2)
FACE OF FEAR (Book #3)
FACE OF MADNESS (Book #4)
FACE OF FURY (Book #5)
FACE OF DARKNESS (Book #6)

A JESSIE HUNT PSYCHOLOGICAL SUSPENSE SERIES
THE PERFECT WIFE (Book #1)
THE PERFECT BLOCK (Book #2)
THE PERFECT HOUSE (Book #3)
THE PERFECT SMILE (Book #4)
THE PERFECT LIE (Book #5)
THE PERFECT LOOK (Book #6)
THE PERFECT AFFAIR (Book #7)
THE PERFECT ALIBI (Book #8)
THE PERFECT NEIGHBOR (Book #9)
THE PERFECT DISGUISE (Book #10)
THE PERFECT SECRET (Book #11)
THE PERFECT FAÇADE (Book #12)
THE PERFECT IMPRESSION (Book #13)
THE PERFECT DECEIT (Book #14)
THE PERFECT MISTRESS (Book #15)
THE PERFECT IMAGE (Book #16)
THE PERFECT VEIL (Book #17)
THE PERFECT INDISCRETION (Book #18)
THE PERFECT RUMOR (Book #19)
THE PERFECT COUPLE (Book #20)
THE PERFECT MURDER (Book #21)
THE PERFECT HUSBAND (Book #22)
THE PERFECT SCANDAL (Book #23)
THE PERFECT MASK (Book #24)

THE PERFECT RUSE (Book #25)
THE PERFECT VENEER (Book #26)
THE PERFECT PEOPLE (Book #27)
THE PERFECT WITNESS (Book #28)

CHLOE FINE PSYCHOLOGICAL SUSPENSE SERIES
NEXT DOOR (Book #1)
A NEIGHBOR'S LIE (Book #2)
CUL DE SAC (Book #3)
SILENT NEIGHBOR (Book #4)
HOMECOMING (Book #5)
TINTED WINDOWS (Book #6)

KATE WISE MYSTERY SERIES
IF SHE KNEW (Book #1)
IF SHE SAW (Book #2)
IF SHE RAN (Book #3)
IF SHE HID (Book #4)
IF SHE FLED (Book #5)
IF SHE FEARED (Book #6)
IF SHE HEARD (Book #7)

THE MAKING OF RILEY PAIGE SERIES
WATCHING (Book #1)
WAITING (Book #2)
LURING (Book #3)
TAKING (Book #4)
STALKING (Book #5)
KILLING (Book #6)

RILEY PAIGE MYSTERY SERIES
ONCE GONE (Book #1)
ONCE TAKEN (Book #2)
ONCE CRAVED (Book #3)
ONCE LURED (Book #4)
ONCE HUNTED (Book #5)
ONCE PINED (Book #6)
ONCE FORSAKEN (Book #7)
ONCE COLD (Book #8)
ONCE STALKED (Book #9)

ONCE LOST (Book #10)
ONCE BURIED (Book #11)
ONCE BOUND (Book #12)
ONCE TRAPPED (Book #13)
ONCE DORMANT (Book #14)
ONCE SHUNNED (Book #15)
ONCE MISSED (Book #16)
ONCE CHOSEN (Book #17)

MACKENZIE WHITE MYSTERY SERIES
BEFORE HE KILLS (Book #1)
BEFORE HE SEES (Book #2)
BEFORE HE COVETS (Book #3)
BEFORE HE TAKES (Book #4)
BEFORE HE NEEDS (Book #5)
BEFORE HE FEELS (Book #6)
BEFORE HE SINS (Book #7)
BEFORE HE HUNTS (Book #8)
BEFORE HE PREYS (Book #9)
BEFORE HE LONGS (Book #10)
BEFORE HE LAPSES (Book #11)
BEFORE HE ENVIES (Book #12)
BEFORE HE STALKS (Book #13)
BEFORE HE HARMS (Book #14)

AVERY BLACK MYSTERY SERIES
CAUSE TO KILL (Book #1)
CAUSE TO RUN (Book #2)
CAUSE TO HIDE (Book #3)
CAUSE TO FEAR (Book #4)
CAUSE TO SAVE (Book #5)
CAUSE TO DREAD (Book #6)

KERI LOCKE MYSTERY SERIES
A TRACE OF DEATH (Book #1)
A TRACE OF MURDER (Book #2)
A TRACE OF VICE (Book #3)
A TRACE OF CRIME (Book #4)
A TRACE OF HOPE (Book #5)

PROLOGUE

Janice tried to turn her head, but it wouldn't move.

She opened her eyes. Her head pounded and she drew breath only with difficulty. She looked around as much as she could without turning her head.

What she saw was enough to make her scream, but when she tried, she found she couldn't do that either. She remained still, her body frozen in a rictus of terror.

She sat at a dining table in a dim room lit only by candles. In front of her and the other four people seated at the table were plates piled high with roast beef, mashed potatoes, and steamed vegetables. A glass of deep red wine sat just ahead and to the right of each plate, and a centerpiece of lilacs and poppies sat in a vase in the middle of the table.

Three of the other four people seated around the table seemed afflicted by the same problem as Janice. They—a man who appeared to be in his late thirties like she was, and another man and woman who looked to be in their late fifties or early sixties—sat ramrod straight, their faces twisted in grotesque expressions of fright. She noticed with a sickening twist of her stomach that they, like her, seemed capable only of blinking and moving their eyes, which they did, flicking them rapidly back and forth.

The fifth person had no trouble moving at all. He held a wine glass up and gestured freely with his other hand as he spoke.

"So I said, 'Frank, if you're going to be like that, then we might as well talk about Mexico City.'"

He laughed and said, "God, you should have seen his face when I said that! You would have thought I had the pictures right there on my phone!" He took a sip of his wine, then said, "Well, I mean I *do* have the pictures on my phone, but I'm not really going to ruin a man's career just because he's a pompous ass. That would be too much."

This man was younger, but not by much. Maybe thirty, give or take a year or two. Absurdly, Janice thought he looked sort of cute. He had a charmingly boyish smile and lively blue eyes. Janice had a weakness for blue eyes.

1

Her skin crawled with revulsion as she realized he was exactly the kind of man she would have flirted with if she'd met him at a bar or a club somewhere.

Then she remembered him. She *had* flirted with him! He had been standing outside the bar she stopped by after work, and she had struck up a conversation with him. Her memory of that conversation was fuzzy, but she recalled wondering if maybe the blue-eyed soul might feel like spending the night with her.

Another wave of revulsion hit her, but she showed no reaction other than to stare in horror. Whatever he'd given her had paralyzed her so all she could do was move her eyes. She struggled to take a breath, but her lungs seemed sluggish and growing more so by the moment.

"Hey Dad," the crazed stranger said, "what do you think about the Phillies this year? We have Turner now, so I think we have a shot at winning the whole thing. Yeah, okay, not a *great* shot, but a shot!" He chuckled. "I'm holding out hope."

He smiled at the older man sitting at the table. After a moment, his smile turned into a frown. "Dad?"

Janice turned to the older man to find his eyes drooped and his lids half-closed. The other two paralyzed victims stared at him in horror, and a moment later, Janice realized why. She tried to scream, but of course, she couldn't.

She drew in a breath, and the difficulty that act presented chilled her, but not as much as the stranger's next words. He sighed in minor exasperation and shook his head. "Looks like Dad's dead. Oh well. I guess I'll have to find a new one."

He stood and walked behind the older man. With a grunt of effort, he dragged the corpse away. Janice tried to see where he took him, but without being able to turn her head, she couldn't.

A few minutes later, the young stranger returned, slightly out of breath from moving the body. "All right," he said, "who's up for a board game?"

CHAPTER ONE

"I didn't have a nightmare last night," Faith said. "In fact, it's been a good two weeks since I've had a nightmare."

"That's wonderful, Faith!" Doctor West asked, "So the meditation is helping?"

Faith shrugged. "I think it's helping to have something to do. I don't know if it's the meditation specifically or just that I have something to focus on other than Trammell, but I'm sleeping better, so I'll take it."

West chuckled. "So the meditation is helping?"

Faith rolled her eyes. "Yes, the meditation is helping."

West laughed again. "You have a very healthy dislike of anything that doesn't fit with your definition of logic."

Faith rolled her eyes again, but smiled. "I guess it's the detective in me. There's an explanation for everything, so when I'm asked to accept something without explanation, I really can't. I don't have a problem with meditation, and like I said, it's helping, whether there's some metaphysical reason or not, but yeah, I don't see myself carrying crystals and asking the universe to send me good vibes."

"I find it interesting that you equivocate meditation with pseudoscience. Do you believe the two are equally laughable?"

"Jesus, Doctor," Faith said, "I just said I don't have a problem with meditation. I notice you have a tendency to get defensive anytime I don't enthusiastically agree with every aspect of your advice. Do you believe that everyone must immediately accept everything you say?"

West laughed at Faith's playful retort. "Fair enough," he said. His eyes twinkled. "I guess it's just the psychologist in me. I always think about what motivates a person's actions. I can't just accept them at face value."

Faith smiled. "I guess you and I share that quality."

"I've always said that psychologists and detectives are two sides of the same coin," West said.

He flipped a page in his notebook and said, "I wanted to follow up on the situation with Michael and Ellie. I understand you still haven't reached out to Ellie to discuss your last encounter."

3

Faith tensed slightly. "No, not yet," she said.

"Not yet as in you'll reach out to her eventually or not yet as in you hope to never see her again and so avoid confronting the issue?"

Faith sighed, "Can we go back to talking about how I don't have nightmares anymore?"

"I'm afraid not," West said, his tone kind but firm. "We're making excellent progress on your PTSD, but I don't see the same progress when it comes to your relationships."

"My relationship with David is going well," she countered.

"I question that," West said, "but we'll talk about David later. Right now, I want to know why you're still avoiding Michael and Ellie."

"I'm not avoiding Michael," Faith said. "I still see him every day at work."

"You're seeing me right now," West said, "but you're still avoiding the question."

Faith sighed. "It's just... I'm not good at..." she searched for a better word, but when she couldn't find any, she finished reluctantly with, "lying to him."

"Why do you feel you have to lie to him?"

"Because I don't like Ellie," she said. "I don't trust her."

"Yes, we've talked about that," West said. "You believe that she's using Michael—you're not sure how—and she doesn't really love him the way she claims to."

"Yes," Faith said.

"And you also agreed that while you may not trust her, you accept that the decision to date her or not is Michael's and that you can let go of your misgivings to allow him his chance at happiness."

"Yes, I know I said that," Faith said, "but I'm having a much harder time letting this go than I thought I would. Michael's my friend, and she's using him. I can't just ignore that."

"So instead, you're ignoring Michael."

"I'm not ignoring him!" she protested. "If he wants to talk, he can talk to me."

"You're trying to deflect the blame for your lack of contact with Michael," West said, "but you've made no effort to bridge the gap either. You're also claiming that it's your concern for Michael that motivates you to talk to him as little as possible."

"I didn't—that's not..." Faith's voice trailed off as she realized that was almost exactly what she had said.

"Faith," West said gently, "you *must* face this issue. You can't run from it."

"So what do I do?" she said, lifting her hands in frustration and letting them drop. "Do I go to him and say, 'Hey, I've tried really hard, but I can't stop thinking about how your girlfriend is lying to you, and I don't think I can be her friend?'"

"Are you afraid that you'll lose him as a friend if you do?"

"Yes!" she exclaimed. "Yes, I am!"

West nodded. "Well, Faith, I won't lie to you. It's very possible that you will lose your friendship with Michael if you confront the issue instead of running from it."

Faith frowned. "And you *want* me to talk to him?"

"Yes," West said, "because I guarantee that if you don't, you will certainly lose him."

They were silent for a moment. "So either I definitely lose him a while later or I possibly lose him much sooner."

"Interpersonal relationships aren't something we can control, Faith," West said. "Other people have free will, and when their wills clash with ours, sometimes that results in a parting of ways. I only know Michael from what you've said about him, but from what you have told me, I feel that if you're open with him, you'll retain your friendship. It will be a different friendship than the one you've had before, but change is something else we can't control, only influence."

Faith sighed. "All right," she said, "I'll think about it."

West smiled. "You're not so great at lying to me either, Faith."

Faith rolled her eyes, but Doctor West chose not to point her reaction out this time.

"So tell me about David," West said. "Things are moving forward with him, yes?"

Faith frowned, "What do you mean moving forward?"

"What do you think I meant?"

"No," Faith said, shaking her head, "you said it, you take ownership of it."

West chuckled. "Using my own words against me. I like it. All right. By moving forward, I mean you accept and allow your feelings for him and feel comfortable pursuing a future with him."

"I wouldn't say comfortable pursuing," Faith said. "I would say willingly considering."

"That's good," West said. "It's a step forward from your previous position."

"You should tell *him* that," Faith said.

She immediately regretted it. West lifted an eyebrow and Faith mentally steeled herself for the interrogation she knew was to come.

"Has he expressed impatience at the pace of your relationship?"

"No, not impatience," Faith said. "Eagerness."

"You don't like that he's eager?"

Faith sighed. "I don't like that we can't just be where we are right now without needing to also think about where we'll be a year from now or what we'll name our kids or do we want more dogs or a cat. Why can't we just enjoy being where we are?"

"You absolutely can," West said, "but you know I'm not just going to leave it at that, right?"

Faith rolled her eyes again, "Yes, I knew the moment I said something that this was going to be a conversation."

"Faith, why do you so detest confronting uncomfortable thoughts and feelings? I used to believe that tendency was only related to the Jethro Trammell incident, but you express strong signs of discomfort and anxiety when talking about anything the slightest bit confusing or uncomfortable."

Faith sighed. "I just... I really don't want to commit to a future when I have no idea what the future can hold. I... I don't know. I don't know if I'm a 'settle-down and marry' type of person. I mean, I *hope* David and I are together forever, but I don't know what might happen that could get in the way of that."

"You don't have faith," West said, "no pun intended."

Faith chuckled. "No, I guess not. I'm more of an evidence kind of person."

"Speaking of evidence," West said, "were you able to dig up anything on the copycat killer when you were snooping?"

Faith frowned quizzically at him. "Since when are you interested in the copycat killer case?"

"I'm interested in you," he said, "and the copycat killer case seems to be the one major boulder in the way of any consistent progress. Not that you haven't made progress. I just feel that your fixation on the case is the most important thing in your life right now, and until you achieve some sort of satisfactory resolution, you won't be able to leave it in your past where it belongs."

Faith nodded. She wasn't sure she followed the leap from being interested in her obsession with the case to being interested in the case herself, but West had surprised her several times already with the information he'd been able to glean from seemingly unrelated threads, so she gave him the benefit of the doubt.

And she did have evidence. Thin evidence, to be sure, but she had found killers on the strength of less.

"I have a suspect," she said, "one the FBI is most definitely not considering."

West blinked, and the surprise on his face was far more powerful than Faith would have expected. She smiled slightly. It seemed Doctor West had more than a professional interest in the case after all. Well, she supposed even psychologists in the Bureau's employ weren't immune to the glamor of a field agent's job.

"Who?" he asked, leaning forward slightly, betraying his interest.

"I can't say," Faith said.

"Really?" he pressed, "not even under doctor-patient privilege?"

"Why are you so interested?" she asked. "Are you planning to conduct your own investigation?"

"Not at all," he said. "I'm just interested in your thoughts."

Faith smiled knowingly. "I think you just want to play armchair detective."

West flushed a little, and Faith laughed. "Ha! Gotcha!"

West rolled his eyes, and Faith said, "I'm sorry, but come on. I sit here every week and endure you picking my brain apart, so knowing that I finally have an insight into Doctor West's enigmatic personality is a victory I intend to cherish."

"Very well," West said, smiling with tolerant exasperation. "I suppose it would be rude of me to deny you this victory. I'll admit, my curiosity is piqued by this case, as is the rest of the nation's. Can you at least tell me how sure you are of this suspect's guilt?"

The alarm on his phone chimed, and a flash of irritation crossed his face. Faith couldn't resist twisting the knife a little.

"Aw," she said, "looks like time's up." She grinned, and seeing West's evident frustration, laughed again. "Not very sure," she said. "I have to do a little more snooping before I can know for sure. You didn't hear me say that, though."

West drew his fingers over his lips in a zipping motion and Faith laughed once more before leaving his office.

West's surprising interest in the case aside, Faith couldn't tell anyone about her suspicions. Not yet. Not until she knew for sure that Clark really was the killer.

It didn't seem possible that a decorated FBI agent could be the man responsible for so many gruesome deaths. Then again, it would make it far more believable that Clark could be so hopeless at finding the killer if he were the killer himself.

Well, that was a worry for another day.

She could be patient. She'd get the copycat eventually. It was only a matter of time.

CHAPTER TWO

"I keep going back and forth on this," she said to Turk. "On one hand, Clark's been a good agent. On the other hand, he's been utterly terrible as an agent on this case."

Turk looked at the tv, which was currently playing a rerun of a cooking show that had been canceled somewhere around the time Faith learned to tie her shoe. He looked back at Faith and Faith said, "Hey, I don't decide the programming. I just pay far too much money for it."

Turk barked, and Faith chuckled. "Well, I'll see if I can find something to rent for you tonight. How about that movie about the dog who rescues all those sick kids? You like that one, right?"

Turk barked assent, and Faith said, "Awesome, sounds like a plan."

She made lunch for Turk, and while the dog happily ate his kibble, she made herself a sandwich. She would be eating with David soon enough, but she could be crabby when she was hungry, and she wasn't in a mood to be crabby on date night.

Turk glanced back at Faith and chuffed before taking another bite of his food.

"It would be the perfect setup, wouldn't it?" she said. "Being assigned to find yourself? You would basically be immune from detection."

Turk barked and Faith smiled. "Unless the world's greatest K9 detective happened to get a whiff of something suspicious. Tell me boy, what did you smell on him?"

Turk shook himself and Faith sighed. "I wish you could speak English."

She fell silent for a moment and considered. It was such a huge leap to suspect Clark of wrongdoing. Still, Turk had lunged at him. He'd only ever done that with suspects before. Even with Ellie, he had only stood in between her and Faith and growled softly when she approached.

Then again, Turk had been wrong before. It was entirely possible he had smelled something on Clark that reminded him of one of the suspects of the Subway Vampire case.

But what would he have smelled? It was equally possible that his intuition, which so far had been flawless in her experience, told him that Clark was a bad person.

She shook her head. This was ridiculous. Clark couldn't be their killer. The whole thing read like a tv movie.

Then again.

She opened her laptop and logged into the FBI's database. She looked up Special Agent Clark. After a few seconds, the screen refreshed to show Clark's smiling face.

"Let's see," Faith said, "Gordon Clark, born January 17, 1982. Joined the Bureau February 22, 2020. Before then…"

She scrolled through his bio and frowned. She could find almost nothing on Clark prior to joining the Bureau. He had graduated from Concordia University in California in 2005, with a bachelor's degree in criminal justice. He had graduated from the FBI Academy on December 16, 2019. After that there was a long list of his assignments and accomplishments as an agent, but between graduating from Concordia and joining the Bureau, there was nothing. No indication of any law enforcement or military experience beforehand. No indication of anything.

It was as though Gordon Clark had disappeared in 2005 and not reappeared until 2019.

Fourteen years was a long gap. Too long. Long enough for Gordon Clark to have created an entirely new identity. Long enough for him to have more than a few skeletons buried in his past. Long enough for someone to have done away with the real Gordon Clark and assumed his identity, then find the perfect career to hide behind if you were planning to be a serial killer.

She closed her laptop. "Now I'm being *really* ridiculous," she said to Turk.

Turk finished the last bite of his food and offered her a noncommittal glance in response. She sighed and finished her sandwich, trying to push her suspicions out of her head.

She couldn't. Her preoccupation—her fixation, as Doctor West would have said—was too strong. She could hope that she was wrong about Clark, but she couldn't just assume that she was. She had to know for sure.

She thought about her next moves. She couldn't investigate Clark. She was being watched, by none other than Clark himself. She couldn't ask Michael to investigate. As her partner, Michael was technically under Clark's authority as well, a fact that further strained their already tenuous relationship. Hell, at this point Michael would be just as likely to report her to the boss as he would be to snoop on Clark.

She thought of her other connections. She had a few here and there as most experienced Special Agents did, but few of them were in a position to be of any help.

There was one person who might be able to assist her.

She dialed a number on her private phone and crossed her fingers that the owner of that number would answer.

A few rings later, a breezy tenor voice said, "Oh my God, miracles do exist. Is this the elusive Special Agent Faith Bold?"

Faith couldn't resist a smile. "Hello, Clyde," she said.

"That's Special-Agent-in-Charge Abel to you," he said in a mock stern tone.

Faith laughed. "Well, hello, SAC Abel."

"Please, call me Clyde," he said.

Faith rolled her eyes. "You just wanted to lord your promotion over me," she said.

"Hey, if I have to manage the most boring field office in the country, then I have to take advantage of every chance for excitement I get."

"Wow," Faith said, "it must be boring if that weak little jab counts as excitement for you."

"Tell me about it," he said. "Ever since you and Prince put the Demon away, it's been crickets here. Even the money-launderers have buried their heads in the sand."

Nearly two years prior, Faith and Michael had been assigned to catch a serial killer who dumped live women into specially prepared wells then tortured them psychologically. He had been named the Demon of Morgan County and his capture was the case that catapulted Faith into stardom.

"Oh come on, it can't be all bad," Faith said. "You get a company car."

"Try driving a front-wheel-drive sedan in a place that measures rainfall in feet," he said, "but enough about me. How have you been?"

"Right as rain," they both said together.

Faith rolled her eyes while Abel laughed on the other end. "Hey, you can't blame me for that one," he said.

"Cheap shot," Faith retorted.

They spent a few minutes catching up before Abel cut to the chase.

"As much as you love me," he said, "I know you didn't just call me to shoot the breeze."

"No," Faith said, "I was hoping you could do me a favor."

"Me?" he said, "do *you* a favor? Wow. Maybe I'll get some excitement after all."

"Well, for both of our sakes, I hope you won't get too much excitement."

"Uh oh," he said. "This is an internal thing?"

"'Fraid so," Faith said. "I need you to look into an agent I work with."

"What's the name?" he asked.

"Gordon Clark."

"Clark? Your supervisor, Gordon Clark?"

Faith's heart sank a little at those words. Apparently, the boss had formalized Clark's promotion.

"Yes," she said.

There was a pause at the other end. "I hate to have to ask why, Faith, but I have to ask why."

"Is this line secure?" she asked.

"I wouldn't even be talking about this if it wasn't," he said. "Go ahead, we can talk freely."

"Good," she said, "I have reason to suspect that Gordon Clark is the copycat Donkey Killer."

Faith heard a sharp intake of breath on the other line. "Jesus," Abel whispered.

"I know it sounds crazy," she said, "and it's going to sound even crazier when I tell you the reason I suspect him, but please hear me out."

"I'm listening."

"So you remember my K9 unit, Turk?"

"Of course I do. He has better instincts than most agents."

"He does," Faith confirmed. "That's why I suspect Clark."

"Turk got a read on him?"

"Yes. He actually lunged at him when Clark approached me in the office."

"Are you sure he doesn't just dislike Clark?"

"No," Faith said, "He wouldn't react that way just because he doesn't like someone."

An uncomfortable memory of Turk lunging at Michael's girlfriend, Ellie, came to the forefront of Faith's mind. She dismissed it, though.

Either that was a fluke, or, as Faith suspected, Turk had reason to dislike Ellie as much as he had to dislike Clark.

"So you think he smelled something that connected him to the case?"

"I think so," Faith said.

"How? If you're not working on the case, what would Turk have smelled?"

Faith took a breath and said, "I have been working on the case."

There was another brief pause. "Ah. This is *completely* unofficial."

"Yes," Faith said, "and I'll understand completely if you can't get involved."

"Faith, the reason I'm an SAC is because of you. I did almost no work on the Morgan County case but got a huge heap of the credit. Whatever you need, I'll make it happen. Still, Faith, this is a serious accusation. Do you have anything at all besides Turk's instincts to suggest that Clark might be involved?"

"Nothing concrete," Faith admitted, "but there's a whole lot of questionable stuff going on. I can't find any information on the man between his graduation from college and his enrollment in the FBI. That's fourteen years of nothing. He graduated from Concordia in 2005 and suddenly became part of the FBI in 2019."

"That doesn't necessarily mean anything, Faith," Abel said. "It's not common for people to join the FBI without a prior background in law enforcement, and it's even less common for people to live so quietly that they have an empty file with the Bureau, but it's not unheard of."

"I know," Faith said, "but he's also a very good agent. At least he was until he took this case. Aside from me and Michael, Clark and his partner Desrouleaux are probably the most effective investigators in the Philadelphia field office. But suddenly, they get handed this case and they get nowhere with it. They're spinning their wheels like they're stuck in the mud with a broken transfer case."

"I get the part about spinning their wheels, but the transfer case thing is beyond my limited automotive knowledge," Abel replied, "and it goes without saying that I'll look into this guy. If you have a concern, that's enough for me. Still, I have to play devil's advocate here. Does your SAC have any suspicions?"

"No," Faith admitted. "I'm just following a hunch."

"Got it," Abel said. "Well, take my advice and stop following the hunch. Let me be the one to follow it. You're on the thinnest of ice right now from what I've heard. Behave, or at least appear to behave, and that ice will thicken rapidly, but right now you're in a one wrong move place, if you know what I mean."

"I know," she said, "that's why I'm calling you."

"Well, you called the right guy," he said. "If this guy's a bad egg, I'll find out."

Faith smiled. She knew that Abel was likely just returning a favor and didn't believe Faith was onto anything legitimate, but she appreciated being trusted enough that someone would at least take her concern seriously.

"Thank you, Abel," she said.

"Don't mention it. If you get a chance, come stop by. It'd be nice to grab a few drinks and catch up."

"Same to you," Faith said.

She hung up and heaved a sigh. With Abel looking into things, she would be able to pull herself away from direct involvement in the case, at least for a little while. Hopefully long enough for the heat on her to die down or for Abel to find something that would obviate the chance of heat in the first place.

She glanced at her phone, and when she saw the time, she jumped and cried, "Crap!"

Turk pricked his ears, and Faith said, "God, I forgot about my date with David! Shoot, I didn't even find a babysitter."

She considered calling Michael but decided against it. Turk would be fine on his own for a few hours as long as Faith left him some food and water. She quickly filled both bowls and changed into an at least somewhat appropriate outfit for a date. When everything was set, she said, "I'll be home soon boy. Don't make a mess, okay?"

Turk cast her a wide-eyed *who, me?* look, and Faith chuckled and ruffled his fur before rushing off.

CHAPTER THREE

Faith poked at her food. The gnocchi, as usual, was delicious, but Faith didn't have much of an appetite tonight. Try as she might to take her mind off of the case, she couldn't stop wondering if Clark really was the copycat killer.

It didn't make any sense, but nothing about this case made any sense. The killer had somehow managed to elude their best agents, Faith included, and left little behind in the way of usable evidence. Rather, he had left a lot of evidence behind, but it didn't seem to point anywhere. Except possibly at Clark, but even that was weak conjecture at best.

She sighed. She had hoped to be able to keep this in the back of her mind now that Abel was helping her, but it wouldn't leave. Like the memory of her time at the mercy of the original Donkey Killer, it was locked in the forefront of her consciousness, like a worm that had wriggled its way inside her and now lay intertwined within the network of her mind.

"Are you listening, Faith?"

Faith blinked and looked up at David, whose typical charming smile was laced with enough irritation to make it appear false and strained.

That meant he was really mad.

"Yes, I'm sorry," she said, "just got lost for a minute."

"That's all right," he said, relaxing slightly. "So?"

His voice trailed off, and after a moment, Faith asked, "So, what?"

David chuckled and said, "What do you think?"

"Umm, I don't know," she replied.

His smile faded slightly and the tension returned to his expression. "You don't know if you like the idea or you don't know what I'm talking about because you haven't heard a word I've said for the past fifteen minutes?"

Faith reddened a little, then took a deep breath and said, "I'm sorry. I just got distracted."

David sighed and his smile disappeared entirely. "Faith, I've been talking to you for fifteen minutes, and you've been responding to me.

15

You acted like you were hearing me, but now I'm asking for your perspective, and you don't even know what I'm asking you for your perspective on."

"I'm sorry," Faith said, "I don't mean to do that. It's just an instinct thing. I have a baseline generic response thing that allows me to seem engaged in a conversation when I'm not actually paying attention. It's very useful in interrogations when—"

"This isn't an interrogation, Faith," David interrupted.

Faith stared at him in shock. He never interrupted her.

"This is a date," he said, "and I would hope I'm worth a little more than a baseline generic response."

Faith reddened with embarrassment and guilt. "You're right," she said, "I'm sorry. I just got lost in my head."

"Yeah, I can see that," David said. "More of the same. This is about the case, right? The one you told me you're definitely not going to interfere with anymore? The one you interfered with more anyway and nearly lost your job over? The one you're allowing to become more important than anything or anyone in your life?"

Faith was so taken aback by this suddenly vehement response that she didn't answer right away. When she did, she stammered and said, "I... I'm sorry. I just... I just fixate on things sometimes, and—"

Once more, David interrupted her. "You know, it would be nice if every now and then, you could fixate on me instead of on a case that doesn't belong to you. You know, just for a moment. Maybe when we're sitting across from each other at a restaurant."

"You're right," she said. "I'm sorry. What was your question? I'll pay attention this time, I promise."

David chuckled bitterly. "I don't think there's a point in asking anymore."

"No, please!" Faith cried out. "Tell me, and I will pay attention this time, I promise."

The desperation in her voice wasn't something she was used to. God, it was like her entire life was falling apart around her.

David looked at her, and she could see the pain in his eyes when he said, "I was asking you how you felt about moving in together."

Faith blinked. Of all the things he could have asked, she didn't anticipate that one.

"I... I thought we decided we were going to wait to take that step."

"Yeah, five months ago," David replied. "I made the mistake of thinking we both felt this relationship was more than just casual. I guess that was a little one-sided."

"No!" she cried out, "no, it's not, it's... David, I'm sorry, I just..."

She cast around for the word but couldn't find it. Finally, David said, "There's always something, Faith. I'm beginning to think there always will be."

"That's not true!" Faith said desperately. "This is just my job! It'll get better soon, I promise."

Her phone rang then, and when she saw the number, she sighed in exasperation. Of course he would be calling her now at the worst possible time.

"You'd better get that," David said bitterly.

Faith sighed and stood up. She stepped outside and answered the phone on the fourth ring. "Bold," she said reluctantly.

"Faith, it's Clark," the caller said.

"Yeah, I know," she said in clipped tones. "Keep it short. I'm on a date."

"Not anymore," he said. "Sorry. There's a case, and the boss wants you on it."

Faith sighed. "It can't wait until the morning? I can look at it first thing."

"Faith, this isn't an office job. It's a field case."

"A field case? I thought I was only doing cheap stuff for now. Cold cases and financial crimes."

"No," he said, "you're still a field agent, and you're still doing field agent work. Get down here. This is a bad one."

"Aren't they all?" Faith replied. "If the boss wants me on the case, then why didn't he call me himself?"

Clark hesitated a moment before responding. When he did, there was a touch of reluctance in his voice. "He wants me to oversee this case as your supervisor. You'll be meeting me in my office. It's the room that used to be storage for all the old copiers and printers."

"Congratulations," Faith said drily. "Prime real estate."

"Faith, goddammit, you did this to yourself. I didn't do this to you."

That remains to be seen, Faith thought. "All right," she said out loud. "I'll be there in twenty."

She returned to the table to see David settling the bill. Her heart sank a little. "David," she began. "I'm sorry."

17

"Don't worry about it," David said. "We were getting nowhere with this anyway. I'll talk to you later."

"I love you," she said.

David paused a moment. He looked at Faith, and there was a hint of sadness in his eyes. "I love you too, Faith.."

But that won't be enough for much longer.

David didn't speak the words aloud, but the sadness in his eyes made the sentiment clear. Faith felt as though a knife was thrust into her chest. She lowered her eyes and tried to think of something else to say, but she couldn't come up with anything. She turned slowly and left the restaurant.

***

She swung by home to get Turk and found Michael waiting for her. "I thought you were at the office," she said.

"I figured we're going to be told to go straight to wherever the hell we're headed after this," he said, "so I thought it made more sense to take one car."

"Makes sense," Faith said. "How are you doing?"

"The short answer is good. If you want a long answer, we'll talk in the car. Come over here, give me a hug."

Faith furrowed her brow but smiled and gave him the hug. "Are you drunk?"

"God, I wish," he said, squeezing her for a moment, then releasing her. "The whole divorce thing has been keeping Ellie and me awake most nights. It's basically like having a second job."

"So she's finally filing?" Faith asked, eyes widening in surprise. She quickly recovered and said, "That's wonderful! I'm happy to hear it!"

Michael offered a slightly tense smile. "Yeah, she's finally filing. I told you she'd get around to it."

Faith felt her own shoulders tense, but she didn't protest. "Well, I want to hear all about the almost nothing I'm sure you'll tell me, but let's get Turk into the car first."

"You're right about almost nothing," he said, and Faith could tell he was serious. "But I will tell you about it."

Ellie was Michael's girlfriend. She and Michael had been dating for nine months, and from what Faith gathered, she had kept promising to divorce her estranged husband without ever taking steps to do that. She had met Ellie once, but her own impression of the seemingly sweet blonde was that she was lying to Michael and didn't feel for him what he felt for her.

That was bad enough, but Turk's impression was far worse than Faith's. Turk had acted nearly as suspicious of Ellie as he had of Clark. He hadn't lunged at her exactly, but he had growled when she tried to touch him, and he had jumped protectively in front of Faith when Ellie had tried to embrace her.

She and Michael had fought often about her choice to trust Turk's instincts over Michael's when it came to Ellie. Faith hadn't made any attempt to influence Michael's relationship, but when he constantly pressed her, she eventually admitted that she felt Ellie was leading him on, though why she didn't know.

She could only hope that this latest news was a sign that she was wrong.

At least he seemed more normal around her this time. There was still tension between them, but he seemed in better spirits than he had in a while. Maybe now that there was progress in his relationship with Ellie, the two of them could repair their own relationship.

In the car—Michael's car, since he preferred the comfy air suspension of his Wagoneer to the stiffer coils of her '96 Crown Victoria—she said, "All right. You promised. I want to hear the almost nothing about the divorce."

"I suppose I did promise," Michael reluctantly admitted. "All right. What I'll tell you is that she and I had a talk, and I asked her to be honest with me about our future. She said she's committed to us, and I told her if that's the case, then she needs to move forward with her divorce. I told her I understand why it's not an easy thing, but she needs to understand that I can't keep waiting for her to figure it out."

"Wow," Faith said, "that's actually not what I expected."

"Not what she expected either. But she understood, and the next week, we went to a divorce lawyer and started the process."

"That's good," Faith said. "I'm glad."

"Me too," he said.

"How long do you think it'll take for everything to wrap up?" Faith asked.

Michael shrugged. "Hell if I know. This is my first divorce. I haven't even seen the ex yet. I assume he's not interested in saving their marriage, since he's made no attempt to contact her at all since we started dating, but who knows? Maybe he'll want to cause trouble just

19

to be a prick. Maybe their finances are still wrapped up in a way that makes him as reluctant to move forward as she is. We'll have to see."

"She hasn't told you about their finances?" Faith asked.

"And that's as much as I feel like sharing," he said.

His hands tightened around the steering wheel and his jaw set. Faith quickly changed the subject to her own relationship in an attempt to break the ice. "Well, if it makes you feel better, I'm in the hot seat with David. I was daydreaming about the copycat case at dinner, and I totally missed it when he asked to move in with me. He accused me of not valuing our relationship. I mean, he didn't come right out and say that, but he might as well have."

"Why would that make me feel better, Faith?" Michael said. "We're not in a competition over whose relationship is shittiest."

"Right," Faith said. "I was just... forget about it."

Michael sighed. "I'm sorry for snapping. I'm not upset with you. But yes, it's probably a good idea for us to drop it."

"Yeah, I agree," Faith said. "Sorry to bring it up."

They remained silent for the remainder of the drive, but when they reached the field office, Michael tossed Faith a knowing look and said, "All right. Let's go talk to the mini boss."

Faith chuckled. "Don't let him hear you call him that."

"Why?" Michael asked. "What's he gonna do? He's not *my* supervisor."

"He is as long as you're my partner," Faith pointed out.

"Yeah, I'll have to work on that," Michael said. "You think if I ask nicely, the boss will let me pair up with Chavez?"

Faith cast a fishy glance at him. Chavez was a new field agent and blessed with unnaturally good looks. "I think you'll have more of a problem with Ellie than the boss if you go that direction."

"Hey, just covering my bases," Michael said. "You could end up being right about Ellie."

"Nope," Faith said, shaking her head. "You said drop it. I dropped it. No more conversation about Ellie."

"Fair enough."

The three of them walked upstairs. The boss—the real boss—wasn't in his office, so Faith didn't have to endure an awkward greeting. They headed to the converted supply closet that served as Clark's temporary office. Faith left Turk in the break room with strict instructions to stay until she returned. She didn't want Turk attacking Clark. Not yet anyway.

20

When they arrived, Clark was standing in front of a small desk that had been placed along one wall.

"Evening, agents," he said. "Welcome to my little slice of Hell. I'd invite you to sit, but I don't even have a chair for myself yet."

"That's fine," Faith said. "I prefer to stand."

"Love what you've done with the place," Michael quipped. "It was a risk to go with less fire, but I think it'll pay off."

"Ha ha," Clark said, unamused. "One day, Prince, you'll have to deal with this shit too, so don't mock me too much or karma will bite you in the ass."

"Not a chance," Michael replied. "The boss will outlive me if for no other reason than to make sure I never make SSA."

"You're probably right about that," Clark said.

"You mind if we get to the case," Faith said tersely, "since it was urgent enough to interrupt my dinner?"

Clark and Michael both turned to her. "Sure," Clark said with equal curtness.

He reached into his desk and pulled a file out, handing it to Faith. "Take a look."

Faith opened the file and held it so she and Michael could see. There were photos of two dead bodies, a man in late middle-age and a woman about twenty-five years younger. Both showed signs of asphyxiation.

"Two victims so far," Clark said, "but we suspect there may be more."

"Why's that?" Faith asked.

"Well, they were both discovered on the same day, both dead from asphyxiation due to carfentanil poisoning."

Faith's eyes widened. "You mean fentanyl?"

"No, I mean carfentanil. As in the same stuff they use to sedate elephants."

"Jesus," Michael whispered.

"In addition to the sedative, they were given pancuronium."

"What the hell is pancuronium?" Michael asked.

"A paralytic. A very strong one."

"So this guy overkilled them twice," Faith said.

"Not sure if it's a guy," Clark replied, causing Faith to roll her eyes, "but yes, that's what it seems like he did."

"Okay," Faith said, "So what else do we know that would cause us to suspect more victims?"

"Both showed ligature marks on their wrists and ankles," Clark continued.

"Why would someone bind people who were paralyzed and sedated?" Michael asked.

"That is one of the questions we expect you to answer," Clark replied, "but if I had to hazard a guess, I would say that our killer tied them upright to a chair."

"You would know," Faith said.

They both looked at her, and she added, "Because of your investigation into the copycat Donkey Killer."

"Right," Clark said. "Anyway, the biggest reason we suspect more victims is that both victims died at around the same time. They were dumped hours apart—the older gentleman in Baltimore and the younger lady in D.C.—but both contained similar concentrations of carfentanil and pancuronium and both were killed at approximately the same time.

"Got it," Faith said. "Are they related?"

"Not even distantly," Clark replied. "The older man is Barret Guiver, sixty-one. The woman is Janice Levant, thirty-nine. They both lived in Baltimore, but on opposite ends of town. Guiver was a foreman at a steel plant and Levant was a department store manager. They almost certainly never met, although that will be something you'll want to look into as well."

"So two people who never met are found dead of similar causes. Clearly the same killer, but why do we think there are more victims?"

"We're not sure yet. We're just preparing ourselves for that event. We can't canvass every dumpster in the DMV, but we're waiting for another phone call if that makes sense."

"So what's our next move?" Faith asked. "Do we go to Baltimore or D.C.? Actually, why isn't D.C. handling this?"

"They are," Clark said. "They asked for you specifically." He glanced at Michael. "And Prince."

"Well, thank you for that," Faith said drily. "So can I get an answer to my question?"

Michael raised an eyebrow at Faith's short attitude but didn't say anything. Clark, for his part, either didn't notice her attitude or—more likely—chose to ignore it. "You're going to Baltimore. Too much red tape in D.C. for you to move freely. You can reach out to the D.C. field office for any of the legwork there. They've made themselves available to you, but I would suggest praying to whatever you believe in that our suspect is in Baltimore and not D.C."

"I'll get right on that," Michael said. "Anything else we should know or is it time to hit the road?"

"Yeah," Clark said. "Time of death was three days ago, but the bodies appear to have been dumped this morning."

"So our killer keeps his trophies a while," Faith said.

"Or he didn't know what to do with them once they died," Clark said. "That'll be another thing for you two to look into. Oh, one more thing: you will report to me daily on your progress. Even if you have nothing to report, I get a phone call. Understood?"

"What?" Michael said. "Seriously? Come on, Clark, this is ridiculous. Can't you just take my word for it that Faith will be good? I'll call you if there are any problems."

Faith frowned in Michael's direction but said nothing. She noted, however, that he asked Clark to take *his* word for it and not hers.

"Sorry, Prince," Clark said, " boss's orders. She reports to me, I report to him daily. I know you're not a part of this, but—"

"I'm still her partner," Michael interrupted. "I'm a part of this."

Clark nodded. "In that case, you two are free to go. Stay wherever you want within reason—FBI within reason, Prince."

"I'm sure I don't know what you're insinuating," Michael said with a sly grin. The boss was still sore at him for running up a multi-thousand dollar expense report at a five-star hotel during the Weed Killer case. "Hey, who's Desrouleaux slumming with while you're playing hall monitor?"

"Boss has him with Chavez for now," Clark said. "Why?"

Michael shared a look with Faith. "No reason," he said. "Talk to you later, Clark."

On the way out of the office, Michael muttered, "Some people have all the luck."

Faith didn't say anything. This case was interesting, and she could grudgingly admit that she was happy to be in the field again, but she couldn't take her mind off the copycat killer case or her prime suspect, the man who was now her immediate supervisor.

CHAPTER FOUR

Faith napped on the drive to Baltimore. Michael glanced over at her once. He felt bad about the tension between them. He wasn't mad at her about Ellie anymore. Now that things were moving forward, he didn't hold a grudge. Faith had made a mistake. She was concerned for her friend, or maybe—though she would never admit this, and Michael would never ask her to—a bit jealous, but he didn't hold that against her. He had to admit that most of his frustration had to do with the fact that, for a while, he suspected Faith might be right.

But she wasn't. The conversation with Ellie had gone well. She was finally proceeding with her divorce. There was no reason for him to be upset.

Still, there was a distance between them now that hadn't been there before. They bantered back and forth like they were still friends, but to Michael it felt more like they were trying to avoid talking rather than trying to bridge the gap between them. They filled the space with noise, but that's all it was. Noise.

He glanced in the rearview mirror at Turk, who sat in between the captain's chairs in the second row of the massive SUV and stared impassively ahead. Michael chuckled. That dog looked more like an agent than some agents.

He held even less animosity toward Turk than he held toward Faith. He was a dog, and like all dogs, he fed off his master's energy. Faith was suspicious of Ellie, so Turk was suspicious of Ellie. Faith resented Clark, so Turk drove him away. It was really just that simple.

What did still frustrate him was Faith's persistent reversal of that belief. In her mind, she was following Turk's instincts and not the other way around. That really was the reason for Michael's earlier resentment over Ellie. From his perspective, she was hiding behind the dog so she wouldn't have to admit her own suspicions.

Well, that was over now. Things were getting better.

And the distance between him and Faith would get better too. It was only a matter of time.

"Watch the road," Faith said, eyes still closed.

Michael looked ahead just in time to swerve back into his lane before a semi plowed into him head-on. The big rig blasted its air horn and Michael said, "Shit. That was close. Thank you."

"Why were you staring at me anyway?" Faith asked. "Reminiscing about old times?"

Michael reddened slightly. He and Faith had dated a while back. Their relationship wasn't as serious as the one he had with Ellie, but before he met Ellie, he had carried feelings for Faith that lasted long after their romance had ended.

"Why are you bringing that up?" he asked irritably. "Are you jealous?"

"Oh come on," Faith said, smiling. "You can do better than that."

"Can we just not talk about that?" Michael asked.

Faith's smile faded. "I was just joking, Michael."

"Well, let's leave the joking aside for a little while," he said shortly.

"Sure," Faith said with equal shortness.

They drove in silence the rest of the way into Baltimore.

It was nearly midnight when they reached the crime scene, a dumpster behind a popular seafood restaurant near a small marina in an upper-middle-class oceanfront neighborhood.

"Why is it always the nice neighborhoods?" Michael complained.

Faith shrugged. "You got me. Maybe rich people go crazy with all that money. Something about all that green."

"There's not even green anymore," Michael said. "Cash is for poor people now. Rich people use credit."

Faith shrugged. "Maybe they just get bored."

Michael let that one pass. They reached the officers waiting near the scene a moment later and Michael and Faith held their laminates.

"Special Agent Michael Prince and Special Agent Faith Bold," Michael introduced them. "This is my partner's K9 unit, Turk."

"Detective Sandra Mickel," the female officer replied. "This is Detective Harris James."

The male officer, a towering man who looked like a powerlifter, nodded somberly at the two agents. Michael thought wryly that a man like that would have come in useful for the Trammell case.

An image flashed through his mind of Faith tied to a chair, bloody and broken under Trammell's knife. He shivered and quickly moved on. "The body still here?"

"No, coroner took it," Mickel said. "I figured that'll be your next stop."

25

"It will be," Faith said. "May we examine the scene?"

"Suit yourself," Mickel said, gesturing toward the dumpster. "There's not much to see. The body was wrapped in plastic, all of which is now in evidence bags at the precinct—your third stop, I assume—and there were no footprints leading to the dumpster. There were, however, traces of the same plastic on the asphalt."

"He wrapped his shoes?' Michael asked.

"Looks like it," Mickel said. "This guy was experienced. We have a feeling there are more bodies out there somewhere."

"That's what we're afraid of," Michael said. "Who found the body?"

"Kyle Kowalski," Mickel said. "Dishwasher for the restaurant. He's sitting inside nursing a coffee." She shook her head. "Poor kid. Not even old enough to drown his thoughts with a drink."

"Can we talk to him?" Michael asked.

"Be my guest," Mickel said. "He wasn't all that coherent with us, but now that he's had a chance to calm down, he might be of more help. You two look nicer than we do anyway. I've always been told I have a mean face."

Michael offered a half-hearted smile, but he wasn't in the mood for banter. Faith appeared to feel the same.

The two of them headed inside and found Kyle sitting at a table near the back of the restaurant. The only other person present was a burly man in an apron and chef's hat who stood next to the boy, arms crossed protectively. He stared at the two agents with a fierce expression, and when they got there, he said in a thick Sicilian accent, "He already talked to the police. They can tell you what he saw. Can he go home please? His mother is worried."

"We'll only be a minute, sir," Faith offered in a soothing voice. "Rest assured, Mr. Kowalski is not a suspect."

Technically speaking, it was too soon for Faith to say that, but one look at the kid and Michael could also tell he was no murderer. He had the wide-eyed expression of shock that Michael knew would likely never completely leave him. An image flashed through Michael's mind of the first dead body he had ever seen, an elderly woman who had died at the wheel of her minivan and plowed into the first floor of his family's home in San Jose. He could still see her filmy white eyes as they stared vacantly at the family portrait that somehow managed to remain hanging on their wall above the smoke rising from her hood.

"Hey kid," Michael said, sliding into the chair across from him. Faith remained standing, but Turk, a born therapy dog if there ever was one, immediately approached Kyle and laid his head gently in his lap. Maybe he could be a trauma support dog once he retired from being a K9.

At Turk's comforting touch, a flicker of life seemed to come to Kyle's face. He took a ragged breath and blinked, and when he did, his eyes weren't so distant. They moved up to Michael's and he began to absently stroke Turk's fur as he regarded the agent.

"Stupid question," Michael asked. "How ya feeling?"

He smiled sympathetically at Kyle. The kid didn't return the smile, but the tension in his shoulders relaxed slightly, and he was able to offer an answer. "I've been better," he said.

Michael chuckled softly. "Yeah. I'll bet. I'm sorry you had to see that. I had a woman plow into the living room of my home when I was a kid. I'll never forget the look on her face."

Kyle shuddered at that, and Faith cast a questioning glance at Michael. Michael ignored it and kept his attention on Kyle. "So, kid. I hate to have to ask you this, but I need you to tell me what you saw. You can hold onto Turk for support if you like. He's a hugger."

Turk lifted his head to press it to Kyle's chest when Michael said that, and Michael thought that, the incident with Ellie notwithstanding, he missed the big mutt a lot. He hoped the two of them—the three of them, including Faith—could spend more time together going forward.

Kyle laid an arm gently over Turk's head. He didn't hug the dog, but he took a deep breath and was far more relaxed when he spoke again. "Um, I was taking the trash out, and when I tossed the bag into the dumpster, I thought I heard a moan. Like someone was inside there. I know that homeless people sometimes go dumpster diving, so I called out, 'Sorry. My bad.' I waited for the hobo to come out, but no one did. I looked into the dumpster because I thought maybe he was hurt, and that's when I saw him."

He shuddered and looked away, holding Turk a little more tightly. "I knew he was dead right away. His eyes…"

His lip trembled and he began to stroke Turk's fur again.

"Yeah," Michael agreed sincerely, "the eyes are the worst part, for sure."

Faith thought privately that the noise would have terrified her more than the eyes. Even knowing that dead bodies often moaned as gases

27

escaped wouldn't do anything to lessen the fright of that sort of experience.

"It's like he was staring ahead at something terrible, you know? Like he could see what was coming after death, and it frightened him. I've never seen anyone look so frightened. I looked down, and he had his hands up, you know, like this." He lifted his hands in a warding-off gesture. "Like he could see what was coming and was trying to protect himself but it was already too late."

"Did you notice any sign of injury?" Faith asked, "Any scratches on his face or hands or any blood on his clothes? Tears, rips, dirt, anything like that?"

"I mean, he was covered in trash," Kyle said, "but that was it. No blood or anything. No scratches either. He just was staring up like he had seen his own death. I don't know, maybe he did."

"Did you notice any kind of footprints near the dumpster?" Faith asked. "Any sign that anyone had dumped him there?"

"I mean, I guess someone had to dump him," he said, "but I didn't see anything."

"The security cameras don't work," the chef volunteered, answering Michael's next question. "He could have been there since the morning or dumped while we were working."

"How likely is that?" Faith asked, "that he was dumped while you were working?"

The chef shrugged. "We take the trash out maybe once every two or four hours. Not often. Sometimes the cooks smoke out back, but usually they go to the porch on the other side of the building. It's shaded, and if business is slow, the patrons don't notice them smoking. So probably no one would have seen anyone."

"What did you do after you found the body?" Faith asked.

Kyle hooked a thumb toward the chef. "I told Chef Pistoli. He called the police."

Michael nodded. "Did you notice anything else out of the ordinary? Anything else that could have indicated what happened to the victim?"

He looked between both chef and dishwasher, but both shook their heads. Michael nodded. He stood and handed each of them a card. "If either of you think of anything, give us a call. We'll be in town for a while."

"Can he go home now?" Chef Pistoli asked. "It's late. His mother will worry."

Michael smiled. "Yes, you're both free to go. Thank you."

Faith called Turk and after allowing Kyle to ruffle his fur once more, the big German Shepherd followed them from the restaurant.

"Our boss could learn a thing or two from Chef Pistoli," Michael commented.

Faith nodded. The two of them returned to the officers and Mickel said, "What did I tell you? Poor kid's scared out of his mind.

"I don't blame him," Michael said. "He didn't see much that could help us either. I learned that the restaurant's security system was down, so the killer could have dumped the body at any time, but most likely it happened before business hours."

"Yeah, we figured," James said, speaking for the first time. He had a deep basso voice that was at once soothing and intimidating.

"You'd make a good drill instructor," Faith mentioned to him offhandedly.

The big detective smiled. "I was. 1st Recruit Training Battalion, 2006-2010."

Faith grinned. "Parris Island, right?"

"Ooh rah," James said. "Embrace the suck."

Mickel smiled sweetly at the two former Marines. "Isn't it cute when two jarheads meet for the first time?"

Michael chuckled. "Young love is the sweetest, isn't it?"

Faith and Harris ignored their counterparts and Faith turned toward the senior police detective. "Is the coroner still awake?"

"Oh yeah," Mickel said. "He'll be pulling an all-nighter with this one."

"Well then," Michael said, "I guess we know where we're headed next."

"Follow us," Mickel said, "it's not like we had anything better to do tonight."

Michael shared a glance with Faith as they walked back to their car. Michael felt the familiar rush of energy that always came at the start of a case. He saw the same excitement in Faith's eyes and felt a touch of hope that the two of them could find a way to be friends again.

"You ready for this, partner?" he asked.

"Always," Faith said.

Turk barked in agreement and Michael laughed. "All right then. Let's go catch a killer."

CHAPTER FIVE

The coroner, as Mickel had predicted, was wide awake when they reached his office, despite the fact that it was after one a.m. when they arrived. The officers introduced them, then called it a night, promising to be available as soon as the agents needed them and to keep them in the loop as their end of the investigation proceeded. Mickel and Michael—God, what a perfect coincidence those names were—bantered like siblings before the detectives left, and Faith thought wryly that Doctor West would have a field day dissecting the reasons behind two hard-boiled detective types partnering with stoic former Marines.

It felt good to be on better terms with Michael, even if the thaw was only work-related. Faith realized that she had been worried the tension between them would impact their ability to work together. For now, at least, that didn't seem to be the case.

The coroner was a thickly built man in his early forties with the harsh sounding name of Horst Steinholz. He stood in between two tables. On one lay the stiffened body of Barret Guiver. On the other, the equally stiff cadaver of Janice Levant. He smiled affably at the two agents and said, "Special Agents, have I got a puzzle for you."

Faith raised an eyebrow. "Oh?"

"Oh yeah," he said. "You probably know about the carfentanil and the pancuronium administered in amounts more than large enough to kill. Here's what you don't know. Those weren't the only drugs our killer gave his victims."

"What else did he give them?" she asked.

"Well," he said, "I don't know yet. But I do know that whatever it was, it allowed our DBs here to survive for days before their hearts finally stopped."

Michael whistled. "Were they paralyzed the whole time?"

"Oh yeah," the coroner said, "Stiff as a board. Or whatever shape our murderer wanted them in. The carfentanil kept their cardiovascular systems calm enough to delay the heart attacks that eventually killed them, but it was whatever the third drug is that kept their hearts beating long enough to keep them from croaking within ten minutes after the carfentanil hit. It probably also kept the pancuronium from paralyzing their diaphragms."

"How could it be so selective?" Faith asked.

"Well," Steinholz said, "there are drugs that only attack voluntary muscles. Actually, pancuronium is an excellent drug for that purpose, but it shouldn't act the way it does here."

"How do you mean?" Michael asked.

"I mean," Steinholz explained, lifting the sheets off the bodies, "pancuronium is a muscle relaxant. As you can see, even hours after death, these two are not at all relaxed."

He prodded at the abdomens of the two bodies and the two agents could see the rigidity in the muscles.

"Our witness at the Italian restaurant stated that he heard a moaning sound escape Mr. Guiver," Faith said, "Is his diaphragm still flaccid?"

"No," the coroner said, "the involuntary muscles stiffened up upon death. You could bounce quarters off their hearts."

"What a lovely image," Michael said drily.

Steinholz shrugged. "Mine is a morbid business, agent. You have to find the humor where you can."

"Fair enough," Michael said. "So can we assume this drug faded before the carfentanil and pancuronium wore off?"

"You can *deduce* that, certainly," Steinholz said, a touch pedantically. "But here's the interesting thing. A few hours before death, the victims received an extra dose of carfentanil and pancuronium. Both of these doses were far more massive than the earlier dose, so these victims actually died of overdose before whatever counteragent our killer used was metabolized."

"So he got impatient?" Faith asked. "Or maybe screwed up the dosage of the mystery drug and had to compensate."

"Maybe," Steinholz said, "I'm not a detective. If I were, though, I would say that it was important to the killer that they survive for a particular event, then once that event was over, he no longer had need of them, and it made more sense to hasten their inevitable demise."

"Was their demise inevitable?" Faith asked.

"Oh yes," Steinholz said. "Their hearts were toast. You can't drug people the way these two were drugged and expect them to survive the ordeal. They were goners the moment the pancuronium entered their bloodstream. Still, our killer definitely kept them alive for a purpose. What that purpose was... well, that requires your expertise."

"Any sign of defensive wounds on the victims?" Faith asked.

"None," Steinholz said. "Needle marks on the insides of both of their right arms where the drugs were injected, and ligature marks where they were tied, but no signs that the victims resisted at all."

"That doesn't make sense," Michael said. "They willingly allowed themselves to be injected?"

"Or they were incapacitated prior to the carfentanil and pancuronium injections," Faith said.

"That's the going theory," Steinholz said. "There are two needle marks and three drugs. So, the mystery was administered a different way, my guess is orally, and had the effect of rendering the victims temporarily unconscious while also greatly mitigating the effects of the other two drugs."

"It seems really complicated," Michael said, crossing his arms. "Why not just knock them out and give them a muscle relaxant to keep them compliant? Why the exotic and exceptionally powerful drugs?"

"Those are detective questions, Special Agent," Steinholz reminded him with a smile.

"We'll visit the first crime scene and see if we can find anything that might indicate where the drugs came from," Faith said. To the coroner, she said, "You have no idea what our mystery drug might be?"

"I'm afraid not," Steinholz said. "Whatever it is, it's not something anyone tests for. It could be experimental or it could be some chemical not typically used as a drug. Either way, I'm reaching out for some help, but it could be a while before I hear something. Actually, if you want to have your offices put some pressure on my sources, it may expedite things."

"Feel free to call the Philadelphia field office," Faith said. "Or the D.C. one. They'll be happy to help."

"I'll do that," he replied. "One more thing."

"Yes?" Michael asked.

"I don't know if this means anything, but he washed, groomed, and dressed both victims before he tied them up."

Faith nodded. "It does. It confirms our suspicion that our killer is finding victims to play specific roles. He dresses them for the role and then once they've played their part, he kills them."

Steinholz nodded. "I see. Well, here's hoping you find this guy quickly. I have a sinking feeling these won't be the only bodies who end up on my table with this mystery drug in their system."

Faith nodded grimly. "I share your concern. I can only hope that we're both wrong."

***

It was close to two in the morning when they left the coroner's office, but neither of them were getting any sleep. Not now.

"What's our next move?" Michael asked.

"Well," Faith said, "we'll want to talk to the victims' families, friends, and coworkers at some point, but that isn't going to happen until the morning."

"We can drive to the dumpster where Janice Levant was found," Michael said.

"In D.C.?" Faith said. "That's over an hour away."

"You have other plans?" Michael asked.

Faith shrugged. "All right. We can go to D.C. You want me to drive so you can get some sleep?"

Michael looked at Faith and said seriously, "I will willingly throw myself into the jaws of a starving alligator before I let you drive my car."

Faith laughed as Michael, as though to emphasize his point, quickly opened the passenger door and gestured for Faith to enter. It felt good to laugh with him. She was still worried about the future of their friendship but so far things seemed back to normal.

At least for a moment. When they drove and the conversation quickly faded, the silence weighed as heavily on Faith as the banter reassured her. In a way, this silence was worse than argument because it wasn't prompted by irritation. They just had nothing to talk about. They had lived so much of their lives apart now, and the only things that had happened of any import were things neither of them wanted to talk about. Michael was obviously not about to discuss Ellie and Faith had no interest in opening the can of worms that was her own relationship right now. She was even less inclined to discuss her therapy. True, her sessions with Doctor West were helping her, but she wasn't interested in talking about it with Michael.

Turk was asleep, so Faith decided to fill the time by reporting to Clark. She hated that she had to report to a man she was increasingly sure was a serial killer, but she hated the empty silence more.

Inspected Baltimore crime scene. Talked to witness and coroner. Third drug present in both victims pending identification by coroner.

33

Killer stages victims to play roles, as yet unknown, then kills them with overdose of carfentanil and pancuronium. En route to D.C. crime scene.

She expected an answer in the morning after Clark awoke so she was surprised when she received an almost immediate response. *Ten-four. Keep up the good work. Tell the coroner to reach out to the lab in Quantico for help identifying the drug.*

Faith hated to admit it, but that was a good idea. She called Steinholz, who agreed to send a sample of the tox report to the FBI lab in Quantico.

Her next call was to the D.C. police department. They agreed to have officers meet the three of them at the crime scene but warned the scene had already been processed and left open to the public. They asked if Faith would rather meet them at the precinct, but she insisted on observing the scene first.

Then she leaned back in her chair and pretended to sleep for the rest of the drive.

They reached the scene at three-thirty. The city was as quiet as Washington, D.C. ever is, which meant that only a few cars remained in the parking garage where Janice's body was found.

"Why would you keep a dumpster in a parking garage?" Michael asked as they walked to the waiting officers. "How is anyone getting a garbage truck in here?"

"I think the garbage men wheel the dumpster to the service lot and dump it there," Faith asked.

"Why not just keep the dumpster in the service lot? Having a garbage truck parked for twenty minutes in the lot isn't going to look any better than a dumpster."

"Washington, D.C. isn't exactly known for making sense," Faith opined.

"Good point," Michael agreed.

They approached the officers a moment later. Turk barked a greeting and the nearest of the officers smiled and saluted him formally before extending a hand, which Faith took. "Sergeant Nicholas Grant," he said in a deep basso voice. "I was the first officer to respond to the call. This is Officer Brandon Kostopoulos. He's my ride for tonight."

Officer Kostopoulos offered a smile that was professional and very exhausted. Faith got the impression this was his first night shift.

"Walk me through the call, Sergeant," Michael said.

"Call came in yesterday morning around six a.m.," Grant said. "A janitor was making his rounds and when he arrived here to dump the restroom trash, he noticed an arm sticking up from the dumpster. Climbed up to take a look and found our victim dead."

"Lovely," Michael said, "bet that was the highlight of his day."

Grant shook his head. "He told us that he had never seen such a look of pure terror on a human face before. Unless he gets paid a lot more than I imagine he does, he won't be able to afford therapy either, so he'll have to deal with the PTSD the rest of his life."

A passing image ran through Faith's mind of a distorted grin with yellow teeth and crazed eyes resting above the smile. Her nostrils flared at the memory of sour breath and her ears tingled. *Let's see how you bleed, little girl.*

Faith ignored the image, following West's advice not to allow those memories power and said, "He reported that Miss Levant's arm was sticking straight up. Did he mention anything else that might indicate she was conscious and capable of movement in the moments leading to her death?"

"I'll let the coroner answer that question," Grant said.

"We already talked to him," Michael said. "Apparently, both vics were fed an exotic drug we don't even know about yet. It kept them alive and aware for much longer than carfentanil and pancuronium should have allowed."

"Lovely," Grant said, shaking his head. "Just what we need. Somebody poisoning people to death slowly."

"Fits the bill for D.C.," Kostopoulos commented, "but they could at least have targeted Congress." He smiled, but when he saw the looks on the others' faces, his smile vanished. "Sorry."

They let the bad joke pass and Faith asked, "Still, did he mention anything specific about Levant's posture? It might be helpful to know when the drugs that our victims were injected with wore off. That might make it easier to identify them."

Grant shook his head. "Just said she looked scared. Terrified, I think, was the word he used. Her arm was sticking up, but to me it looked like she was just dumped as she was."

"So she was paralyzed in that position."

"That's my best guess."

Turk put his nose to the ground and began sniffing. "Maybe your K9 can pick up the scent and find the drug for us," Grant suggested.

"It's happened before," Faith said.

Michael's lips thinned slightly, but he didn't say anything. In their last case, Michael had suggested that Turk had misidentified the chemical phenol several times when they were looking for suspects. In fact, he had smelled the phenol but also smelled bleach and it was the competing smell that had confused him.

Still, in the end, he had found their criminal. Faith thought that Michael secretly resented that he wasn't able to identify the killer and prove Faith was mistaken to trust the dog's instincts.

Whatever the case, he didn't make an issue of it now.

Turk sniffed around the dumpster but trotted back to them without reacting to anything. If there was a smell here, it was a smell Turk didn't associate with a killer.

"What can you tell me about Janice Levant?" she asked.

"Thirty-nine, managed the department store in this mall. Single, no kids. Parents live in Pensacola. I imagine you'll want to talk to them."

"Yes," Faith said.

"I'll give you their contact information. We haven't had much of a chance to investigate yet. Just a quick phone call to her parents and her former employer. We heard from all of them that she was a friendly and kind person who got along well with everyone. Honestly, that could mean she was friendly and kind or it could mean she was a wallflower, and no one noticed her. I don't need to tell you that."

"We'll talk to her employer anyway," Faith said. "You never know what you might dig up."

"True," Grant said. "Other than that, there's not much I can tell you other than that her only prior was misdemeanor possession back when she was in college. Marijuana and MDMA. Molly, we called it back in those days."

"I'm surprised that's still on her record," Faith said.

"Officially, it isn't," Grant said, "but when someone is murdered, we have access to things we otherwise wouldn't."

Faith didn't want to get into a debate over the morality of reviewing expunged criminal records. Besides, she didn't really have a leg to stand on when it came to moral behavior in law enforcement.

"Any witnesses?" Faith asked. "Besides the janitor?"

"A few people who showed up after the janitor called me. Heard the commotion and came down to see what was up. Left with a story and nothing else."

"What about the security cameras?" Michael asked. "Anything from those?"

"The precinct is still reviewing footage, but we may not find anything. The camera only covers the right half of the dumpster. Theoretically, our killer could have dumped her through the left side and left without ever exposing himself to the camera."

"Lovely," Michael said. "Why the hell do people even invest in security cameras?"

Grant shrugged. "Appearance. If you can make people think they're safe, then that's enough to keep the money flowing. Keeping people actually safe is secondary. No one expects to find a dead body in their dumpster."

"And yet it happens," Faith pointed out, "every day."

Grant nodded sympathetically. "If only the world would behave exactly as we want it to."

"It would make a lot of things a lot easier," Faith said.

"Do you have contact information for her employees?" Michael asked.

"We do," Grant confirmed. "I'll give you our file. Most of the information is stuff we've already sent your bosses, but it does include contact information for the victim's family and her employees."

"We'll look into it," Michael said. "Thank you, officer."

"Don't mention it," Grant said. He smiled somewhat bitterly and said, "Another day in the life, right?"

"God bless America," Michael deadpanned.

They decided to spend the night in D.C. Or rather, they decided to stay at a hotel in D.C. and enjoy a short nap before getting started on the case again.

As usual, day one had provided them with very little in the way of usable information. The victims were both drugged and bound, kept alive for a few days, and then murdered and dumped. Both contained lethal doses of carfentanil and pancuronium and a sizable dose of a mystery drug that combined with the other two and kept them alive long enough for the killer to enact whatever sick fantasy he or she dreamed up.

Past that, they had absolutely nothing in common. Different jobs in different cities. Different ages, different genders. Both Caucasian, but that didn't really narrow anything down.

Once more, nothing made sense.

Well, they would make sense of it. After all, that was their job.

Just before turning in for her nap, Faith sent two texts. The first, to David, read *Thinking of you*. The second, to Abel, read *Update?*

Faith was somewhat displeased to find she anticipated Abel's reply more than she anticipated David's.

CHAPTER SIX

The alarm clock went off at six-twenty-one, as it did every morning. Except Sundays. He allowed himself to sleep in on Sundays, although he rarely slept past seven even when he wasn't working.

Today, he was working, so he rolled over and tapped the snooze button, then stretched out and waited for the nine-minute snooze timer to run out. When the alarm clock sounded again, he sighed and rolled out of bed.

"Another day, another dollar," he repeated with a chuckle.

He got out of bed and got ready for work. By seven-thirty, he was showered, his teeth brushed, his hair combed neatly, and wearing his ironed and pressed uniform. He smiled at his reflection and said, "Looking dapper today, Danny!"

His name wasn't Danny, but Dapper Dan always struck him as a smart nickname. Smart. That was one of Dad's favorite phrases. He used it to mean intelligent, of course, like everyone else did, but he also used it to mean something particularly pleasing or well-fitting. Dapper Dan was a pleasing and well-fitting nickname.

His smile widened. He really was a smartly dressed, Dapper Dan of a man. Mom would be proud.

He practically bounced into the kitchen. Mom was waiting there, along with his older brother and sister. They were in town visiting for a few weeks, but he was pretty sure he could convince them to stay. After all, what better place to live than the center of the greatest democracy in the world?

"Good morning!" he said cheerfully, waving at them. "Sorry I can't stay for breakfast. I have to put the order away before we open for business."

He looked around and frowned. "Where's Dad?"

His family didn't answer, but their faces registered shock at Dad's absence. They sat perfectly still, comically alarmed at the absence of the family's patriarch.

"Oh, relax," he said, flipping his hands. "You three are always so worried. Dad's probably just on another of his long walks. I'll find him."

His family didn't answer, but he thought he detected a note of relief on his older brother's face. He always acted like he was the only responsible one in the family. Well, that was all right. At least he wasn't a jerk anymore like he was when he was younger.

He left for work, a smile on his face.

He reached the parking lot less than ten minutes later. The lot was already nearly full. He checked his watch and was relieved to find he was twelve minutes early.

"If you're ten minutes early, you're on time," he whispered. "If you're five minutes early, you're late."

That was another of Dad's favorite sayings. He thought sometimes that Dad had never left the fifties, which was odd considering Dad was born in fifty-nine, and his childhood was spent in the loving sixties and the chilled-out seventies.

Well, Dad always did admire Grandpa.

He parked and started toward the employee entrance. Just before he entered the building, he looked up and saw Dad. "Ah!" he said, "there you are!"

Dad was too far away to hear him. He was checking the hours sign at the entrance. He chuckled as he started over toward him. Silly Dad. Why didn't he call and ask him to let him in early? He could do that for family.

Well, no matter. He'd show Dad the VIP experience, and when work was over, he'd give him a ride home.

He checked his jacket for the syringes. All three were present.

His smile widened, and when he approached his father, he lifted a friendly hand and called, "Hello, sir! Can I help you?"

CHAPTER SEVEN

Faith checked her phone. More nothing. Faith was getting tired of nothing.

No response from David to the follow-up text she had sent yesterday. From Abel, the only response was *Nothing yet. Will contact later.* After a moment, she sighed irritably and tossed the phone onto the table. Turk, who was napping in between the two beds, pricked his ears up but slowly lowered them without opening his eyes.

"Well, that's another lot of nothing," Faith muttered, voicing her thoughts.

Day two had been as fruitless as day one. More so. At least on day one, they had learned about the mystery drug. Today, they had only confirmed that neither of the victims was connected in any way and furthermore established that both were the salt of the Earth and had no enemies that might have a motive to kill them. Janice Levant's family, in particular, had been shocked that anyone would want to hurt someone as kind and loving as Janice.

"She's just such a giving person," her mother had lamented to Faith. "How could anyone do this to her?"

Faith didn't have a good answer. Come to think of it, she didn't have any answer at all. Or rather, she did, but she didn't imagine Mrs. Levant wanted to hear that there was no reason, none that would make sense, anyway. Some people were just evil or broken. Some people were both. Some people just wanted to tie people to chairs and cut them with rusty knives to see how they bled.

Janice's employees echoed the same sentiment as her family. She was a good boss and a kind person, and they couldn't understand how anyone could hurt her like that.

A few worried that they might be targeted next. Faith offered the lame reassurance that they were doing everything they could to find the killer and bring him or her to justice and dispensed the pointless advice to lock their doors and windows and avoid being outdoors alone, but with no idea what their killer's profile or motives were, she couldn't in good conscience tell them that they were safe.

She reached the hotel in a bad mood and upon discovering that Michael's investigation into Barret Guiver's circle had been similarly fruitless, her mood worsened. Now, well past midnight and still unable to sleep, her mood was as low as it had been since learning that the boss knew of her interference in the copycat Donkey Killer case. That discovery had nearly cost Faith her job and had put her on probation, meaning that she had to report to the man who was now her number one suspect in the Donkey Killer case.

Her phone buzzed, and she snatched it quickly, heart leaping with excitement. That excitement disappeared almost immediately.

It wasn't David or Abel. It was Clark. *Update?*

She sighed and rubbed her temples with her hands. She texted back, *Nothing new to report, will update when I have a lead.*

A moment later, Clark replied, *What leads have you followed up on today?*

Faith's irritation grew. She took a deep breath and typed, *If you can read, you'll know that I have no leads and will contact you when I do. Back off.*

She stared at the text for a moment, indulging in the fantasy of being able to say that to him, then erased the message and sent a perfectly compliant response, *Spoke to family and coworkers of both victims. No apparent connection or possible motive. Currently searching for connections between them.*

A minute later, the phone buzzed. A thumbs-up emoji.

Maybe it was just Faith's exhaustion, but that emoji incensed her. Like she and Clark were what, buddies now? Like they were in this together?

She knew she was being ridiculous, but the whole situation grated on her. Ten years of experience with the bureau and she was being babysat by a man who at best had less than a third of her experience and at worst was the serial killer she had fixated on for over a year now.

To make matters worse, Michael was returning from his snack run and Faith could hear snippets of his conversation.

"Whatever you want, Babe, seriously," he said, laughing. "Come on, do you *really* want me to decide how we decorate the kitchen?"

She heard the beep of the door as Michael slid his keycard into the lock, and a moment later, he stepped inside, straining to keep from dropping the shopping bags in one hand while he held his phone to his ear with the other. He set the bags down on the table just next to where

Faith worked, and she gritted her teeth as he laughed and said, "I mean, if you're okay with pictures of guns and airplanes. Maybe I can mount that longhorn skull we saw at the fair last month."

He continued to laugh and banter with Ellie, and Faith's lips tightened. It would be just her luck that, despite her beliefs about Michael's relationship and her own, Michael and Ellie would live happily ever after and she and David would end before they ever even got started.

Dammit, why couldn't the boss just give her the copycat case? All her problems would be solved if he just gave her the case and let her get that monkey off of her back.

Michael hung up and said, "All right. I got you pinot noir, as you requested. I also got chips, trail mix, and peanut butter cups."

"I didn't ask for peanut butter cups," she said.

"Those are for me," Michael replied, "Not everything's about you."

"My mistake," Faith said flatly.

Michael ignored her tone and said, "Anything new?"

"No," she said, "Why would there be anything new? I've been sitting on my ass for the past hour. How would there be anything new?"

"I think you need some sleep," Michael said, finally showing some of his own irritation. "I'm just asking. Why don't we get some rest and reapproach in the morning?"

"Because we don't know where to begin in the morning," Faith said, sighing and rubbing her temples again. "I don't want to keep looking over the same pieces of evidence."

"I think we have to, Faith," Michael said. "We need a fresh set of eyes, and since we're the only eyes available, we need to let our eyes freshen before we look at this again."

"Excellent advice, Doctor," Faith quipped.

"All right," Michael sighed, sitting next to her. "Since you obviously have a bug up your ass, fine. Let's brainstorm some more. What do we know?"

She lifted her hand and let it drop. "Two victims, different in every way, found in dumpsters drugged with the same cocktail of poisons."

"Well, that's something," Michael said. "We know this guy dumps his victims in dumpsters after keeping them for a while. He's clearly keeping them for a while before he kills them."

"Whoop-de-do," Faith said. "How does that help us?"

"I don't know, Faith," Michael snapped. "I'm just trying to keep a positive attitude."

Faith sighed and said, "You know what, you're right. I'm sorry. We need rest."

"Yeah," Michael agreed. His phone buzzed, and he stood and answered. "Hey, Babe. Give me a second to step outside. No, she's fine. Just tired. It's been a long day."

Faith's lips thinned again. Now they were talking about her. Wonderful.

She changed for bed and wondered what her dreams would have in store for her tonight. She rarely had nightmares anymore, but the early stages of a case always seemed to bring with them a fresh crop of bad dreams.

Tonight was no different. No sooner did sleep reach her than the familiar dream arrived. Once more, she was tied to a chair at the mercy of Jethro Trammell, the Donkey Killer. Once more, she promised herself fruitlessly that she wouldn't allow him the satisfaction of hearing her scream. Once more, he approached her with a crazed gleam in his eye, but this time he didn't hold a rusty knife.

This time, he held a syringe. The little wheeled tray that stood a few yards away no longer held rusty tools and cutting implements but instead held two other syringes along with three vials. Two of the vials were labeled clearly: CARFENTANIL and PANCURONIUM. The label on the third was smudged.

Faith tried to struggle but found she couldn't move, not even within the limits imposed by the cords that bound her hands, feet, and chest to the chair. Her body was completely rigid, paralyzed except for her eyes, which strained to keep Trammell in their field of vision as he approached.

Trammell smiled down at Faith and said, "Time to play, little girl."

He reached forward and Faith felt the needle slide into her skin. He depressed the plunger, and she felt the cool liquid enter her vein and travel rapidly toward her heart.

She took no comfort in the fact that she couldn't scream.

***

"We have a suspect," Mickel announced proudly.

Prior to this revelation, Faith's nearly sleepless night had left her groggy, but at this announcement, she jumped instantly to full alertness. She glanced at Michael to see he had also shaken the cobwebs.

"Where are you?" she asked Mickel.

"Precinct B," Mickel replied. "Lucky for you. That'll shave fifteen minutes off your drive."

"We're on our way," Michael said. "Forty-five minutes."

Mickel chuckled. "You'll be lucky to make it here in an hour, Special Agent, but I admire your zeal."

She hung up and Michael grinned at Faith. "See? Things are looking up."

"Let's not get our hopes up too much yet," Faith cautioned.

She grinned as she said it, though, and both of them were in a better mood as they navigated the road to Baltimore.

As predicted, it took an hour for them to reach Precinct B, despite its favorable location at the extreme southern end of Baltimore. Faith noticed wryly that Michael still took time to stop for coffee at the precinct's break room before meeting Mickel and James. Not that she could judge. She poured herself a cup of coffee and savored the first sip with relish as they made their way to the waiting detectives.

"What do we got?" Michael asked when they reached the detectives.

"Felix Maynard," Mickel replied, "fifty-four. Former Congressman for North Carolina, resigned in scandal after paparazzi caught him with three college girls in his limo. At the same time, too. Gotta hand it to the guy. He has a lot of energy for an older dude."

"What's his connection to this case?" Faith asked.

"Well," Mickel said, "I'm not sure if there's a connection yet, but we do like him for the murder of a prostitute we found in a warehouse dumpster this morning."

Faith raised an eyebrow. "Has the autopsy been completed yet?"

"No, it's happening now. Steinholz is under strict instructions to call the moment the tox report comes back."

"Perfect," Faith said. "Is Maynard here?"

"He's here," Mickel said. "He's marinating in interview room three. Denies everything of course. Insists he won't talk to us until his lawyer gets here. All the while talking almost nonstop." She shook her head. "No wonder he got caught sleeping around. The guy's a blabbermouth."

"Has he blabbered anything interesting yet?" Michael asked.

"Not yet," Mickel said, "but I'll bet dollars to donuts we'll have a full confession by the time the morning is out."

"I'll take that bet," Michael said.

"Can we talk to him?" Faith asked.

"Be my guest," Mickel said. "You look like his type. Maybe he'll be more inclined to talk to you."

Faith's stomach turned at the joke, but she kept a polite smile on her face as Mickel led them to the interview room. She knew that many people turned to humor as a way to deal with the stresses of the job. Hell, she had done the same before Jethro Trammell had taught her that there was no humor at all in a world inhabited by monsters.

The former congressman was, as promised, ranting up a storm in his cell.

"You can't hold me here!" he cried out, "I have rights. I have..." He turned toward the agents and said, "Who the hell are you? How is this an FBI case?"

"Good morning, Congressman," Faith said. "I'm Special Agent Faith Bold and this is Special Agent Michael Prince. We need to ask you some questions."

"I have nothing to say!" the congressman thundered. "So unless you're planning on calling my lawyer, you can just forget about it!"

Faith pulled up a chair and set it down in front of the congressman, then sat, staring at him. He glared back defiantly, but there was a good deal of fear in his stare as well.

Fear and guilt.

Faith maintained her gaze and after a moment, the congressman fell silent. When he did, Faith said, "I'll cut right to the chase, Congressman. We're investigating the murders of Barret Guiver and Janice Levant. They were found in dumpsters two days ago. From what I understand, your victim was also found in one as well."

"Not my victim!" he insisted. "This is outrageous!"

Faith thought wryly that that his thundering tone must have served him well in Congress. Not well enough to cover up his penchant for cheating on his wife with college kids, but hey, you can't win everything.

"Michael," Faith asked, "will you please ensure that the congressman's lawyer is on his way?"

"Her way," Maynard corrected.

Faith raised an eyebrow in mock approval. "Look at you," she said, "hiring a female lawyer. Is she pretty?"

"I don't have time for this," Maynard said. "Am I being detained?"

"Yes," Faith answered. "The police obtained security footage of you dumping a body into a dumpster."

46

"Must be hard having to do so much on your own these days," Michael said. "No one on the payroll to cover up your mistakes."

"I didn't murder anyone!" Maynard insisted. "She left me in perfect health. What happened after that is none of my concern!"

"So you *did* sleep with her," Faith said. "Do the detectives know that?"

Maynard paled. "I'm not saying another word without my lawyer!"

"I'll follow up on that," Michael said. "You have her phone number? Her office, I mean. I'm sure you have her personal number."

Maynard reddened at the insinuation but managed to keep from slipping further. "I gave it to the detectives," he said. "They denied me my phone call."

Michael smiled. "I'll make sure she knows where you are."

He stepped outside and Faith said, "Mind if we chat while we wait?"

"I told you," he said, "I'm not answering any questions until she arrives."

"That's fine," Faith said. "I'll talk, you listen." She smiled. "I tend to think out loud anyway. Having a good listener present helps me organize my thoughts. Are you a good listener, Congressman? I'm guessing you are since you seem to be so popular with the ladies. Although I guess the money and power thing probably meant a little more. Boy, it sucks not to have that anymore, doesn't it? Then again, when you pay a girl, you don't have to worry about making sure she enjoys it."

The congressman glared sourly at Faith with an expression that looked pathetically like an insolent child's pout.

"So we know about the prostitute," Faith said, "that makes sense. She probably tried to extort you, right? Thought she hit paydirt and promised not to tell your ex that you were still seeing hookers if you hooked her up. Then she found out that your star faded long ago, and that she had hitched her horse to the wrong wagon. I imagine it pissed her off. After all, she would never have agreed to do all those things with you if she had known you were washed up. Probably decided she was going to tell baby momma anyway. Things are already bad enough between you and your daughter. I imagine this latest revelation would make them decide against letting you have a relationship with your grandkids."

"That—" Maynard began.

He clammed up immediately, and after a brief pause, Faith said, "What doesn't make sense is Janice Levant and Barret Guiver. Why them? I mean, Guiver was a staunch Republican, but I can't see you killing a man for voting the other way. Janice was a little old for you—after all, she was only sixteen years younger than you—so that doesn't make sense either. Did she cut you off on the Beltway?"

"This is ridiculous," Maynard said. "You guys are jokes."

"Maybe," Faith said. "Maybe we are. You know what isn't a joke? Murder."

"What?" he asked.

"This is bullshit!" he cried. "I don't know about carfentanil or pancuronium or murder. Look, I..."

His eyes shifted to the left and Faith's own eyes narrowed. She leaned forward and the smile vanished from her lips. "Congressman, I strongly suggest you don't lie to me right now. News media loves stories about disgraced former congressmen caught murdering prostitutes. Your face is going to end up on national television. Hey, then again, maybe that's what you've always wanted."

"My lawyer..." he began shakily.

"Is on her way," Faith said, "and if you think she can get you off, you go ahead and talk to her. Who knows? Maybe she'll keep the CIA from making you disappear."

"All right!" he hissed. "Look, I don't know anything about carfentanil or pancuronium, and I don't know anything about Janice MacGyver or whatever the other guy's name is. Look, we..." he sighed. "We did heroin, okay? I shot her up so she'd be... relaxed. She had a reaction, and... I didn't know, okay? She had needle tracks all up both arms. I thought she'd be able to handle the dose. But I didn't kill anyone else okay? It was an accident! Dammit, it was..."

His voice trailed off. He looked down at his hands and said, "It was an accident. We were just supposed to have fun. She wasn't supposed to get hurt."

Faith watched him for a moment. She looked at Turk. Turk regarded Maynard carefully but didn't react otherwise. Faith turned toward the two-way mirror and nodded. A moment later, the two officers came in, followed by Michael.

The lawyer arrived ten minutes later. After the usual bluster about a confession under duress and unlawful detainment, she allowed the detectives to show her the security camera footage which clearly showed a harried-looking former congressman dumping a woman's body into a dumpster behind a warehouse.

Maynard had alibis for the night of Guiver's and Levant's dumpings, so the agents had to settle for the silver lining of solving this case.

Clark was not enthused. "That's all well and good, Faith," he said, "but I need results on the case you're working now. If we're right about this, then we're going to see more bodies pop up soon. Work this case, Faith. You're not getting anywhere with the victim angle. Start looking into the drugs. See if you can find a connection that way. Do some detective work."

Faith bristled but kept her voice under control. "Yes, sir," she replied. "I'll report again tonight."

Clark hung up and Faith and Michael said their goodbyes and left the precinct. Faith shared Clark's advice about pursuing the drug angle and Michael said, "Works for me. How about we do some digging over breakfast?"

"Suits me," Faith said.

On the way to a nearby café, Faith felt a moment of sympathy for the victims. They hadn't been used in the same way as the woman the congressman murdered, but they had been used, nonetheless. They had lives and families who loved them, but all of that had mattered less to one sick individual than his desire for... whatever it was he was doing.

Maybe the killer, like the congressman, felt lonely and instead of finding a healthy form of companionship he chose to use drugs to force others to be what he wanted them to be. It would explain why the victims were found paralyzed with ligature marks that indicated they were tied up prior to death.

Then again, maybe there was no "logical" motive.

Some people just like to see others bleed, she thought as Michael pulled to a stop in front of the Lazy Daze Café.

CHAPTER EIGHT

He chuckled and shook his head. His poor dad. You couldn't take your eye off him for ten seconds. He invited him inside to get the family treatment and go behind the scenes with the animals, but Dad was confused again. He refused and then wandered off to a nearby coffee shop!

Well, that was okay. He'd feel better after he had his medicine.

He felt in his pocket to make sure the syringe was still there. His finger grazed something sharp and blind panic slithered through his veins for a moment before he realized he had only touched a rough spot on the plastic and not the tip of the needle. He laughed and he didn't like the waver that came to his voice when he said, "Ha! Imagine that. Overdosing on your dad's medicine. Wouldn't that be a headline?"

He glanced around nervously, but there was no one within earshot. The lizard in the back of his brain, the one that had slithered in through his fear, told him that he needed to be more careful. He couldn't have outbursts like this in public.

And he couldn't carry the "medicine" without putting the syringes in a case or a bag first. It meant being more careful about retrieving the syringe when he took someone, but he could manage. He couldn't risk being caught, and he definitely couldn't risk killing himself with his own drug.

He took a breath and released it slowly. When he did, he looked up and saw Dad sitting inside the café with a newspaper in his hand.

The lizard in his brain slithered away to wherever it lived when it wasn't scolding him. He chuckled and smiled in patient exasperation. That was just like Dad. He had a perfectly good cellphone, a perfectly good tablet, and even a laptop, but he still got his news from an honest-to-God paper.

He walked inside and ordered a coffee. He decided to sit a few tables away from Dad while he waited for his coffee. Why not let the old man enjoy his peace for a moment?

A moment later, however, Dad got up to use the restroom. He sighed and stood. Dad would never admit that he needed help, but he did, especially when he didn't take his medicine.

His medicine! He could give Dad his medicine in the bathroom! That would be good. Dad got paranoid without his medicine.

He entered the restroom, and, as predicted, found Dad standing in the middle of the room polishing his glasses, as though that were the most important thing he could be doing in a restroom.

"Dad, you're a hoot sometimes, you know that?"

Dad jumped when he spoke and looked at him with a startled and confused expression. "Jesus!" he said. "You scared the hell out of me!"

"Sorry Dad," he said, lifting his hand and smiling. "Just wanted to make sure you're okay. You kind of wandered off on me."

Dad peered more closely at him and said, "Hey. You're that weirdo from the gate, aren't you? Hey, what the hell are you doing here? Are you following me?"

He sighed. Poor Dad. He really needed his medicine.

He pulled the needle from his pocket and smiled patiently at Dad. "It's okay, Dad," he said gently. "You just need your medicine."

Dad's eyes widened. He drew in breath to scream. The lizard in his brain shouted *NOW!* and he lunged forward, lips twisted in a snarl.

Practice made perfect. He drove the needle directly into the man's jugular vein. He knew he had injected the drug before he had a chance to scream, but he still covered his mouth, just in case. He kept his hand in place until the man's eyes rolled back in his head. Then he pulled the older man into his arms and carried him into the closest stall.

Now what?

This was the first time he had taken someone in public. Everyone else had come from his workplace. There it was easy. He knew where to go, how to move without being seen. He had a perfect cover there that made it effortless. No one even looked.

But this was different. How could he get out of the bathroom? People had seen both of them go inside. They would notice if one of them came out thrown over the other one's shoulder like a bag of rice.

The door to the bathroom opened, and he froze. He looked underneath the stalls and saw a pair of walnut brown loafers walking slowly in his direction. He looked down at his own feet and saw that the elderly man's feet sat next to his.

He drew in a deep breath, careful not to make any noise, and with an effort, lifted the man until his feet weren't visible underneath the stall.

And of course, the newcomer had to go number two.

51

He took deep breaths and slowly widened his feet to brace himself as he held the older man up. He was strong and trained to carry people, but this was far from an ideal position, and he'd never had to carry a person for more than a few seconds. His arms began to shake and beads of sweat formed on his brow.

Finally, the stranger left the bathroom, and with a sigh, he lowered the old man back to the ground.

He needed to move. They would see them leave together, but he thought it would be less suspicious to have one pair of feet in one stall and not two pairs.

The lizard cut through the panic and reminded him that, in all likelihood, that fine gentleman didn't give—pardon the pun—two craps about who was or wasn't in the restroom at the same time as he was. *You just need to move and not make a scene. You can manage that can't you?*

"I can manage that," he said softly.

He moved the old man, supporting him with one arm. He moved one of the old man's arms over his shoulder and held it with the hand not under the man's armpits. He took a breath and steadied himself, then left the restroom.

He chuckled and said in a low tone, "All right, Dad. Let's get you home."

A few people glanced his way, but none looked past his apologetic smile. More importantly, no one noticed that the old man's feet dragged rather than walked or stumbled.

When a few gazes did linger longer than he felt comfortable, he explained, "Dad has narcolepsy. He'll be okay. We just need to get him home to rest."

The semi-curious patrons nodded acknowledgement and quickly returned to not caring at all.

He walked to his car and calmly placed the man in the passenger seat, moving carefully and without rushing. The hair on the back of his neck prickled, and it took every ounce of his willpower to keep from glancing around to make sure no one was watching; the lizard reminded him that doing so would make him look far more suspicious.

He got into the driver's seat, started the car, and pulled smoothly into traffic. He maintained his nonchalant demeanor until he pulled onto the freeway. Then he took a deep breath and released it in a shuddering sigh.

"Whoo," he said, "that was a close one. You gotta stop scaring me like that, Dad."

His father didn't answer. He glanced over and saw him flopped to one side in the seat, his head lolling forward on his chest. He chuckled and shook his head. Of course Dad would put him through that and then the very first thing he does is take a nap.

His phone rang, and he jumped and cried out. He reddened with embarrassment and looked sheepishly out of his windows. No one had seen him.

He answered the phone. "Hello?"

"Where the hell are you? You were due back from lunch half an hour ago."

His smile disappeared. Work. He was supposed to be at work.

The lizard crawled out of its hole and took over. He smiled again, even though no one was there to see him. People could hear smiles. He'd known that since childhood. "Hey, Bob, I'm sorry I didn't call you. My dad's having a bit of a health scare, and I have to go check on him."

"Oh God," Bob said, his tune changed completely at the news. "Oh, I'm sorry. You take all the time you need."

"Thank you," he said apologetically. "He's probably just freaking out. Every time he feels a twinge in his side, he thinks it's a heart attack, but you know old people. He's probably just overreacting."

"Oh," Bob said, relaxing a little. "Well, all the same, go ahead and take the day. Can't be too careful with these things."

"No, definitely not," he said. "Thank you, Bob."

"No problem. You take care."

"You too."

He hung up and took a deep breath. Once more, that was too close. He couldn't forget about work. That was a *major* no-no.

He would have to get back on a schedule. He didn't want to be so regimented about it, but he couldn't risk days like today. He needed to be more careful.

He looked through his windshield at the clear blue sky. The sun was already warm despite the early hour. If he looked closely, he could almost see the flames rippling and seething on its surface.

He rolled the windows down just slightly to allow some of the fresh air inside for Dad.

It was going to be a beautiful day.

CHAPTER NINE

"And none of these substances would interact with carfentanil and pancuronium in a way that would produce the effects I've described?"

"No," Doctor Langevin replied. "Frankly, if you have carfentanil, none of these other drugs are necessary. People use carfentanil to sedate elephants."

"Yes," Faith said, "that's what I've heard. Well, thank you for your time, Doctor."

"Of course, Special Agent. If there's anything else I can do for you, let me know."

Faith smiled at him, but her smile disappeared the moment she and Turk walked outside. She called Michael and when he answered, she said, "Tell me you have some good news."

"I wish I did," Michael said. "I'm guessing that means you don't have any good news for me."

Faith sighed. "Nope."

"Nice," he said. "Well, I guess we once more know where not to look."

"I think we check out zoos next," Faith said. "I've done some research, and it looks like they use carfentanil and pancuronium to sedate large animals."

"Are there zoos besides the National Zoo?"

"Probably," Faith said, "but we'll start with the National Zoo."

"Wonderful," Michael said. "You want to tell the mini boss or shall I?"

Faith sighed and closed her eyes. "I'll call. He's supposed to be keeping tabs on me."

"I would say I'm not grateful that it's you on the hotseat and not me, but damn, am I grateful."

"Thanks, buddy," she said drily.

"Pick you up?"

"No, I'll take the transit. Maybe I'll get lucky and Turk will just happen to run into the killer again."

Michael laughed. "Stranger things have happened."

"To us? Definitely."

Michael laughed again. "I'll see you back at the hotel."

Faith took a breath and let it out slowly as she walked to the bus stop. She would call Clark on the bus. She was in no hurry to have that conversation. She made it halfway there when her phone rang again.

Detective Harris James.

"Bold," she said.

"Special Agent, we've received a call you might be interested in."

"What is it?" she asked.

"Abduction. An eyewitness saw an old man dragged out of a coffee shop by a younger man. Said the younger man called the older one Dad and put him in the passenger seat of his car."

"How did she know it was an abduction?" Faith asked.

"She said the old man was unconscious when he left the coffee shop and his feet were dragging on the floor. The younger man had to load him in the car seat."

"I'm on my way," Faith said. "Do we have an ID on either of them yet?"

"We're working on a sketch right now," James said.

"Wonderful," Faith replied. "Get me the address. I'll be there ASAP."

As soon as she hung up, Faith called Michael. "Michael, come pick me up."

"Seriously? Faith, I'm already on the Beltway—"

"Michael, there's been an abduction of an elderly man from a coffee shop. Eyewitness says a younger man carried an unconscious older man out of the shop and loaded him into his car, then drove off."

"Jesus," he said. "Okay, I'm on my way."

They reached the coffee shop thirty minutes after James's phone call. The eyewitness, an older woman with an apron who Faith guessed to be the owner of the shop, waited with James and Mickel.

"Agents, welcome," James said. He turned to the older woman. "These agents will speak to you briefly, ma'am and then you'll be set to go."

"Okay, thank you, Detective," the older woman said. She played with her apron strings and shivered, clearly unnerved by what she had seen.

Michael removed his coat and offered it to the older woman who accepted it gratefully. "I'm Special Agent Michael Prince, ma'am. This is Special Agent Faith Bold."

"It's a pleasure to meet you," the older woman said with habitual politeness. "My name is Ariadne Hollister."

"What a lovely name," Michael said with a smile.

Ariadne smiled a little wider and relaxed a little. "Thank you, young man," she said, her voice a little stronger and steadier now.

Turk trotted over to her, tail wagging, and that sealed the deal. Ariadne's shoulders relaxed and her smile softened. She reached down to scratch Turk behind the ears, a movement the latter greeted with evident pleasure.

Michael smiled again. "Miss Ariadne, will you please tell us what you saw?"

"Yes," she said, nodding. "Of course. I was working at the cash register, covering for my employee who was on lunch break, and I saw a younger man carrying an older man out of my shop. It looked like the older man was unconscious. His head was slumped forward and his arm was limp and his feet were dragging on the floor."

She took a shuddering breath and Turk leaned gently against her and looked up at her with his perfectly empathetic gaze. Ariadne calmed again and said, "I tried to tell myself that it wasn't what I was seeing, but then he put him into his car like he was a package. I don't think that older man went willingly."

Tears welled in her eyes and Michael grabbed her hands. "Hey," he said softly. "It's okay. We're going to find him."

She took a deep breath and smiled, relaxed once more. Faith looked away. It was true that they would find him, but the chances of him being alive when they did weren't high.

"Did you know either of these gentlemen?" Michael asked.

Ariadne shook her head. "No, I had never seen them before."

"Can you describe them for me?"

"Well, the older man, he was around my age, sixty-five or so, and he had white hair. He was a White man, about five-foot-six, a little paunchy, if you know what I mean. He wore a corduroy sweater with a golf cap and black penny loafers. I thought he was very smartly dressed. I wonder why no one wears corduroy anymore? It's so comfortable."

Faith and Michael shared a glance. Aside from the different clothing, this victim sounded similar in build and appearance to Barret Guiver.

"And the younger man?" Michael prompted.

56

"Well, he was very fit," Ariadne said. "Not like a bodybuilder, but like a construction worker or a fireman. Not so rugged though. He had very boyish features. You could think he was in high school if it weren't for the stubble. He wore some sort of uniform, but I didn't catch where it was from. It looked like a nurse's outfit."

Faith and Michael shared another glance. This could be their first real lead.

"Hair color?" Michael asked gently. "Eyes?"

"Oh yes, blonde hair, blue eyes. Very Scandinavian."

"Did he interact with anyone else while he was here?" Faith asked. "Either of them?"

"Well, with me when they paid for their order. With Cassandra when they picked up their order. Cassie didn't say anything about them to me one way or the other, and I thought they were very polite, especially the younger man. Oh, if only I had known!"

She buried her face in her hands and Michael laid a comforting hand on her shoulder. "Hey, hey," he said softly. "This isn't your fault. And we'll find them, okay? We're very good at it. Especially Turk here."

Turk chuffed in agreement, and Ariadne smiled again. "Thank you. I just can't believe this happened! People used to be decent. Now, with all the drugs and the violence all over the internet—" she shook her head "—Everything's just so insane! That's what it is. It's insane!"

Faith and Michael shared a final glance. Michael kept a comforting hand on her shoulder but said nothing.

After ensuring that Ariadne was safely on her way home, the two agents conferred with the officers.

"Best guess is he followed the older victim into the bathroom, incapacitated him there, then left, probably trying to pass the older man off as his father. Evidently, it worked."

"We need an ID on the victim quickly," Faith said.

"We'll put out a bulletin," Mickel promised. "All we have right now is the sketch to go on, but odds are plenty of people will start calling relatives. We'll get a lot of false alarms, but eventually, one of those alarms won't be false."

"That could be too long," Faith said. "He only keeps them for a few days."

"We're aware of the ticking clock, Special Agent," James said. "We'll do our best."

Faith nodded. "Has CSI found anything useful from the bathroom?"

James shook his head. "Footprints and fibers from all sorts of clothing, too many to positively identify any one of them as belonging to our killer or our victim, even with Ms. Hollister's description."

Faith sighed. "Yeah, I figured. Well, if you manage to find anything useful, let us know."

Michael and Faith left the officers to work and headed to another nearby café for breakfast. While they sat over their coffees and muffins, they brainstormed.

"So we've confirmed that he does have a profile," Faith said. "We don't know of another Caucasian woman in her late thirties yet, but that's two Caucasian men in their sixties."

"He's building a family," Michael said.

Faith nodded. "Possibly. Probably. Definitely something along those lines."

"So what do we think?" Michael asked. "Is he going to wait until he finds a woman that fits his profile or will he start in on the old man first?"

Faith grimaced. "What a lovely way to describe it," she said, drily.

Michael shrugged. "My question still stands."

"Yes," Faith said, "it does. Honestly, I don't know. It's possible he already has a female victim." She pulled out her cellphone and opened her Bureau VPN-protected browser. "I'm going to look through the missing persons cases," she said, "see if anyone fits the profile."

"You do that," Michael said. "I'll look through the police blotter and see if there's anyone on the hook for kidnapping or human trafficking."

Faith lifted an eyebrow and Michael asked, "What? My straw's not as graspable as your straw?"

Faith shrugged. "Grasp away."

They ordered more coffee and four scrambled eggs and a bowl of water for Turk. While Turk ate happily, Faith and Michael pursued their individual lines of investigation.

Faith expected to have to search for victims who fit her profile. The opposite turned out to be true. She found thousands of active missing persons cases, hundreds within the past month and dozens just in the past week. No fewer than twenty-one of those cases fit the description of a Caucasian woman of average build in her mid-to-late-thirties with brown hair and brown eyes. Only four of the missing persons were Caucasian men in their sixties, but none of them fit their profile or the sketch of their victim, so that didn't help Faith at all.

She sighed as she browsed through the descriptions. Her investigator's instinct told her that most of these cases would resolve themselves over the next few days, but they only had a few days to begin with.

She passed the information along to Detective Mickel, and Mickel promised to look into those cases but warned Faith what she already knew. It was likely that they would either have no leads or that the leads would turn out to be unrelated to the case.

Well, as long as they were grasping at straws, it was better than nothing. Only just better than nothing, but still better than nothing.

"Got something," Michael said.

Faith's ears pricked up. "What is it?"

Michael came around the table and showed Faith the file he had pulled up. The face that greeted Faith was unkempt and hardly boyish, but he had blonde hair and blue eyes and, to a woman in her sixties, a man in his forties could look boyish. This was promising.

"Who and what?" Faith asked Michael.

"Pyotr Koszinsky," Michael replied, "Polish transplant. Did eleven years in Florence for human trafficking. Got out in 2011, then returned in 2013 for six years. This time it was a prostitute he kept chained in his house for three weeks until she bit through her ropes and got a neighbor to call the cops."

"What a peach," Faith said.

"Bet he makes his mother proud," Michael agreed. "He fits the description, and best of all, he lives in Fort Meade, conveniently halfway between D.C. and Baltimore." He looked up at Faith. "What do you think?"

Frankly, Faith thought he was unlikely to be their killer, but they had no other leads. This was just enough of a possibility that it was worth investigating. "All right," she said, "let's go pick him up. Does he have a workplace?"

"Garbage man," Michael said.

"They don't do background checks anymore?" Faith asked.

"I imagine there's not a long line of people waiting to be garbage men," Michael replied.

"Fair enough," Faith conceded. "Call the waste management company and get his route. Maybe we can find his truck."

"On it."

While Michael called, Faith settled the bill. Pyotr's route at this time of the day was a residential neighborhood in the hills a few miles behind them.

On their way, Faith thought of the old man who was now likely tied to a chair, paralyzed, and frightened, waiting for whatever crazed psychopath had brought him there to decide he was finished with him and kill him like he did the last one.

Let's see how you bleed.

Her eyes narrowed and though she didn't say the words aloud, her mind offered the same rebuttal she gave every time Jethro's taunt surfaced in her mind. *You first.*

Despite her bravado, Faith worried that their killer may be too far ahead of them. Their last killer had evaded them long enough to kill twice more. She could only hope it wouldn't happen again.

CHAPTER TEN

Michael decided that from now on, he would ask for a cruiser when they investigated. He was pretty sure they had hit every single damned red light in Baltimore on their way to the route.

Faith was quiet again, but Michael couldn't tell if it was focus or doubt that kept her that way. He wasn't particularly excited about this lead himself, but it was a lead, and they couldn't afford to dismiss anything at this point, no matter how far-fetched it was.

And it wasn't that far-fetched. Pyotr's appearance skirted on the edge of the description provided by Ariadne Hollister, but his priors fit the profile, and murder was a natural escalation from trafficking people then kidnapping them and holding them captive.

It wasn't the best of leads, but it was good enough to be worth their time. And he was desperate to do *something*.

He would never admit it aloud, but lately he felt a little like the third wheel for Faith and Turk. Turk would find the clues and Faith would crack the case. Michael was little more than a driver and the cleanup crew when Faith found the criminal.

He despised himself for his jealousy, but there it was anyway. He wasn't Special Agent Michael Prince anymore. He was Special Agent Faith Bold's partner, her sidekick. He wasn't proud of feeling this way, but part of him hoped Pyotr was their man because if he could solve a case and not just sit around while Faith solved it, then he would have more confidence in his own abilities. He wouldn't have to feel jealous or insecure around Faith and that confidence might help repair the damage done to their friendship.

The light in front of them turned yellow just too late for Michael to make it. He sighed irritably and pressed the brake, stopping just before the light turned red.

"Next time, we're getting a patrol car," Faith said.

"Agreed," Michael said. "Remember Tucson? That was the business. We could get anywhere in the county in fifteen minutes. Good times."

Faith shrugged noncommittally. "I wasn't a fan of the people," she said.

Michael chuckled. "I thought you liked the younger one, what was his name?"

"Derek," Faith said, "and he was cute, but I don't go for cute. I like rugged."

"Is David rugged?" Michael asked.

"He is where it counts," Faith replied.

The light turned green, and they fell silent. The banter eased the tension somewhat, but as they approached the street where they expected to find Koszinsky, the tension took over. Michael turned the corner and saw the truck halfway up the street. "Showtime," he said.

Faith drew her weapon and Turk stood, growling as he prepared to go after the suspect. "We'll try to get in front of him," Michael said. "Stop him before... dammit!"

Without warning, the garbage truck suddenly sped forward. Michael hit the gas and the SUV leapt forward. The twin-turbo six-cylinder engine allowed them to easily outpace the garbage truck, but the truck had too much of a head start. It pulled out of the neighborhood and onto the main street before Michael could reach them.

"Dammit!" Michael swore again.

Faith called nine-one-one to report the chase, but with no lights on his car, Michael had to drive very creatively to keep up with the truck, which barreled down the road at speeds that were shocking from such a big vehicle.

"Units are on the way," Faith said. "They'll be here in... Michael, watch out!"

Without warning, the garbage truck swerved to one side, then the other. The sudden movement unbalanced the vehicle and it slowly rolled over onto its side, sliding to a stop across all three lanes of traffic.

Michael slammed on the brakes and narrowly avoided becoming part of the pileup that rapidly formed behind the vehicle. They came to a stop fifty yards from the truck and quickly jumped out.

Pyotr climbed from the driver's seat of the garbage truck, evidently unharmed by the accident. He slid down the other side of the truck and bolted.

"Turk, get him!" Faith shouted.

The dog bolted after Pyotr, quickly outstripping the human agents. Pyotr turned, and when he saw the dog following him, he ran to the opposite side of the street, weaving dangerously through oncoming traffic. Turk was smart enough to run down the side of the street blocked by the garbage truck, but when he came alongside Pyotr, the latter cut through an alleyway in between two buildings, leaving Turk stuck behind the moving cars.

Michael swore and sprinted across the street after Pyotr. Faith ran toward Turk and began to halt traffic so the dog could cross safely.

Michael drew his weapon and called out, "Pyotr Koszinsky! FBI! Stop!"

He reached the alley to find no sign of Koszinsky. He swore again, but a moment later, Turk rushed past him, Faith hot on his heels. The dog must have picked up the scent of garbage.

Michael ran after them, trusting Turk's nose to lead them to Pyotr. He hoped desperately that Turk wasn't simply leading them to a dumpster.

How had he known they were FBI? Had someone tipped him off from the waste management office?

It was possible. Michael doubted Pyotr was the only ex-con they employed. He wanted to believe that most of the convicts were genuinely rehabilitated, but it only took one bad apple to sour the whole bunch.

Turk trotted in and out of the alleys that crisscrossed the small shops lining the street, but after a few minutes, he stopped and sniffed the ground. Michael caught up with Turk and Faith and the latter shared a grim look with him.

In the distance, they could hear sirens as the police finally approached. Faith called dispatch and instructed the officers to form a perimeter around the area. He couldn't have gone far.

He wouldn't have to go far. He could hide indefinitely if he knew the area well enough, and since he was a garbage man, he definitely knew that area. They could and probably would bring more K9 units to help Turk, but if the scent of garbage was all they had to go on, then they would just end up in the same damn place.

Then Turk lifted his head and barked. Michael's eyes snapped to where Turk looked. He was staring into a café across the street. Michael peered in through the window and saw Pyotr, looking nervously out the window at Turk. He tried to remain casual as he stood and sauntered toward the restroom, but when he saw Michael and Turk rushing after him, he sprinted, shoving past an employee and a patron on his way to the restroom.

Turk sprinted toward the door, Michael behind him. They rushed into the restroom just in time to see Pyotr's legs disappear out of the window. Turk leapt through the window and Michael heard Pyotr cry out when the dog landed on the other side.

"Hold him!" Michael cried, climbing through the window.

He saw Turk hanging onto Pyotr's arm, struggling to drag the suspect to the ground. He pointed his weapon through the window and called, "FBI! Stop or I'll shoot!"

Pyotr looked at him and grinned. "Shoot me then," he said, lifting his arm so that Turk's body interrupted Michael's shot.

Michael hadn't planned on shooting Pyotr anyway, but he didn't like that Pyotr had called his bluff. This man was dangerous.

He could hear Faith shouting behind him and called back, "He's outside! He's behind the coffee shop!"

Pyotr's smile disappeared when he heard Faith approach. With a snarl, he threw Turk to the ground, wrenching his arm free. Blood trickled from the wound, but he took no notice of it and sprinted off down the alley.

Michael pulled himself through the window and jumped down, but his foot caught on the windowsill and he landed heavily, smacking his head on the pavement hard enough to see stars.

"Michael!" Faith called, rushing to his side.

"I'm all right!" Michael cried. "Get Pyotr!"

He heard a low growl as Turk rushed off after the suspect. A moment later, he heard Pyotr cry out again. He sat and waited for his head to stop swimming. When his vision cleared, he saw Pyotr on the ground, Faith on top cuffing him, and Turk standing near his head, snarling, and glaring at him.

Pyotr unleashed a stream of profanities at Faith and Turk and when Michael approached, he included him in his soliloquy.

Faith stood him up while Michael called the officers to inform them of the collar. When he finished, he smiled at Pyotr. "How's the arm?" he asked genially.

"Fuck you!" Pyotr returned.

"Thanks," Michael replied, still smiling, "but I'm married."

Pyotr rolled his eyes, which Michael decided was fair.

***

"Lawyer," Pyotr said, glaring daggers at the two agents. Turk growled at him, and he grinned and lifted a finger at the dog. He couldn't lift his hands very far since they were chained to the table, but he managed to get his point across.

"Of course, Mr. Koszinsky," Michael said, "do you have a number you'd like us to call?"

"You're supposed to give me a lawyer," Pyotr said.

"Once you're charged with a crime, the court will appoint a public defender," Michael agreed, "but you haven't been formally charged yet. We're just having a conversation."

"Well, we can have a conversation with a lawyer," Pyotr said. "I've been here before, Agent, I know my rights."

"You have been here before, haven't you?" Faith said. "How old was the girl you kidnapped? Eighteen? Nineteen?"

Pyotr grinned at Faith. "How old are you?"

Faith's lip curled in contempt and Pyotr laughed. His laughter ended in an abrupt glare, and he repeated, "Lawyer."

"Of course," Michael replied. "Do you have an attorney?"

Pyotr sighed and rolled his eyes. "Look, I can sit here all day. You can get me a lawyer or you can watch me sit here."

"Here's the thing," Michael said, taking the seat across from him. "We have hundreds of eyewitnesses who saw you crash a garbage truck in the middle of a busy street and run from FBI agents who identified themselves to you. One of those witnesses is Robbie Gaussman. You know Robbie? He was your partner. He was on the truck with you when you rolled it over. You'll be happy to know he's going to be okay. The doctors were able to save his leg, so he'll be back on his feet right as rain in no time."

Pyotr glared but said nothing.

"He had some interesting things to tell us," Michael said. "For instance, he said that when you saw our car, you said, 'Fuck those cops,' and gunned the engine. He said you refused to explain how you knew we were law enforcement and why you were running. You ignored his repeated requests to stop the vehicle, and he also said that just before you rolled the truck, you said, 'Yeah? Check this out.'"

"Essentially, Pyotr, we have more than enough evidence to convict you for reckless driving, aggravated assault with serious bodily injury on your friend Robbie, a whole litany of criminal and I'm sure civil charges for the many people you hurt in the pileup, not to mention all the damages that come from the cars involved."

"So we can wait for you to find a lawyer and get them over here, in which case, you will absolutely be charged for all of these crimes; or you can talk to us, and if you tell us something we like to hear, maybe we can help reduce some of the criminal charges."

Pyotr laughed bitterly. "You can't reduce shit. This is my third strike. I'm going to prison for life no matter what happens here, whether I help you or not. I told you, Agent. I've been here before. You can't bluff me. I either help you and go to prison for life or I don't help you and go to prison for life. Well, I'm not in a very helpful mood, so how about you go ahead and formally charge me and when my ten-cent-an-hour public defender shows up to convince me to take whatever deal you want to make, I'll tell him the same thing I'm telling you."

Michael leaned back in his chair and sighed. Pyotr was right. He was in prison for either the rest of his life or long enough to mean the same thing whether he talked or not, and of course, if he talked and they could pin the murders on him, he'd be looking at a shorter stay, ending in a lethal injection. There was no benefit to talking that Michael could see.

After a moment of silence, Faith said, "You're right, Pyotr. You're going to prison for the rest of your life. Well, maybe not. Depending on what we find out about you, you might only get twenty-five years. I won't pretend we're going to be able to make any kind of deal with you that's going to reduce your sentence, but I will tell you that not talking to us is going to determine what kind of sentence you're looking at."

"You just said you can't reduce my sentence," Pyotr said.

"True," Faith replied, "but there's a big difference between serving time at Florence and serving time at Cumberland Camp."

Pyotr's smile faded. He took a deep breath and ran his hand over his forehead. "If I talk to you, I'm as good as dead no matter where I go."

"Not true," Faith insisted.

Pyotr laughed again. "If I rat on them, they'll find me. They'll find me whether you put me in Cumberland, Florence, or Guantanamo Bay. They'll have someone kill me. If you think people can't sneak weapons into Florence, you're naïve as shit. Not that they would need to sneak a weapon. They'll probably just pay another lifer a carton of cigarettes to sharpen a toothbrush and hide it in my temple."

Michael frowned and shared a look with Faith. "They?"

66

"The others," Pyotr said. "You guys always had it wrong about me. I'm not a captain. I'm not even a lieutenant. I'm a foot soldier. They don't put the higher-ups on the street. They put assholes like me on the street, people who don't have money or families. They make it damned clear that if we squeal, they'll find someone to kill us wherever we go. Kill us bad. They'll do it too. I saw them off three guys in Florence. Guards didn't do shit."

"Pyotr, are you telling us that you're still involved with human trafficking?" Michael asked.

Pyotr looked between Michael and Faith. Finally, his eyes settled on Faith. "You promise me you can get me protective custody? You can keep me out of GP?"

"I can't promise anything," Faith said, "but our word carries a lot of weight with the FBI, and since this is a federal case, there's a very high chance we can get you somewhere you won't be harassed."

Pyotr hesitated a moment longer until Faith said, "It's no chance at all or some chance. It's up to you."

Pyotr hesitated a moment longer. Then he sighed and leaned back in his chair. "All right." He took a breath and said, "Here goes. About a year back, I was approached by one of my former contacts with the Bulgarians. He asked if I was interested in running some product for him."

"Product?"

"You know, girls."

"Right," Michael said, his lips curling in disgust.

"Well, I told him I wasn't really looking to get back into the life, but he… insisted." He looked seriously at the two agents and said, "These aren't guys you say no to. They pay people to come from Bulgaria to kill someone, then flee the country. Sometimes they don't kill you right away. That's not counting all the other soldiers they have over here. I didn't have a choice."

Faith adopted the same contemptuous expression as Michael but kept her voice professional. "So you agreed to traffic individuals for what I'm guessing is the Bulgarian Mafia," she said.

"I don't know if they call themselves the mafia," Pyotr replied, "but sure. Same shit I did before."

He fell silent, and when Faith raised an eyebrow, he said, "That's it. I don't know the names of the girls I took. They were all hookers anyway. I didn't go after anyone with a life or a family that might look for them. I learned my lesson about that the last time."

"Besides the girls," Michael asked, "who else did you take?"

"That's it," Pyotr said, "just girls. They don't pay for boys anymore. They source 'em locally. Girls from America are considered exotic, especially dark-skinned girls. I went mostly for them."

Faith looked at Michael. She pulled the photos of Barret Guiver and Janice Levant from her pocket and placed them on the table in front of Pyotr. "So you don't know who these two individuals are?"

Pyotr looked at them and shook his head. "Nah, I never killed anyone. They don't pay for dead people. Besides, the woman's too old, and like I said, no one pays for boys anymore. Even if they did, that man's obviously way too old."

Michael looked at Faith. Faith shook her head slightly. He sighed and stood from his chair.

"So that's it?" Pyotr asked. "That's all your questions?"

"I'm sure the police will have more for you," Faith said, leaving the room.

Michael and Turk followed her. Michael conferred briefly with Mickel and James. The officers, though disappointed at making no progress on Faith and Michael's case, were understandably excited to have broken open a human trafficking case. Faith and Michael managed to hide their frustration until they left the precinct.

Outside, Michael sighed and swore bitterly.

"Don't beat yourself up about it," Faith said. "I thought he was a good lead too. It's like you always say. Detective work is a whole lot of nothing and then everything all at once. This is just part of the nothing we have to wade through."

Michael managed the ghost of a smile as Faith called Clark to update him. While she was on the phone, Michael pulled a cigarette from his pocket and lit up. Ellie would kill him if she knew he was smoking and Faith would no doubt have some choice words for him herself.

Michael couldn't care less about that right now. Once more, he had proven useless. True, it could hardly be called a total failure to have apprehended someone involved in a human trafficking ring connected to organized crime, but it was Faith who had gotten the perp to talk. If she hadn't been there, they would have been waiting for official charges and a lawyer and weeks or months of courthouse struggles; by that time, Michael would have been long gone from the case anyway.

He tried to remind himself that it wasn't about personal success or accolades but about putting bad guys behind bars. The more he

68

reminded himself of that, the hollower it sounded in his ears, so he finally just gave up and allowed himself to feel like crap.

"Smoking again?" Faith asked.

"Whatever," Michael groused.

Faith stiffened but let it drop. After a moment, she said, "We'll get this guy, Michael."

"Yeah," he said, "I'm sure we will. In the meantime, we once more have a whole lot of nothing, and I'm going to be pissed about it for a while."

"Be pissed about it if you need to be, but don't let it get in the way of your job," Faith exhorted him.

Michael met her eyes and asked, "Are you sure you want to talk about emotions getting in the way of our job?"

Faith bristled again but didn't reply. Michael turned away. He felt guilty for his comment. Faith was only trying to encourage him. He just wasn't in the mood to be encouraged right now.

He looked outside at the sun, halfway toward the western horizon. He took a drag on his cigarette and contributed another puff to the haze that obscured the sky and sighed heavily.

What a shitty day.

CHAPTER ELEVEN

Faith checked her phone. Still no response from David. She had sent three more texts, one each day since the first text went unanswered.

She sighed and slumped in her chair, staring blankly ahead at the wall. Turk sat in between the two beds, watching an old kids' movie about two dogs and a cat who are separated from their family on a camping trip and have to find their way back. Michael was in the shower, his breakfast, like Faith's left mostly uneaten.

She wished David would call. She hadn't realized before how much she valued having him. At home, she thought of him more as a fun diversion than as a serious part of her life. She cared for him, of course, but time with him was time to stop thinking about the future and the dangers and disappointments it held.

She knew that was a large part of what was driving them apart now. He wanted Faith to commit to him for a long-term relationship, and she wanted to avoid anything that would require more effort from her. She wished now that she hadn't been so closed-off. No doubt David was convinced that she didn't want a future with him.

Frustration rose, and her breathing quickened. She wanted a future with him, but why did they have to talk about it now? Why couldn't they just let it happen? I mean, God, did she need to pick out wallpaper now? When they were still in the honeymoon stage?

She took a deep breath and let it out slowly. Doctor West would say that Faith's reluctance to discuss commitment was out of fear: fear that she would put effort into building a relationship only for it to fail or fear of admitting that she didn't want a lifelong connection with David, meaning she lost out on the time they could have had.

Maybe that was true, but Faith didn't think so. Simply put, she just didn't want to have to work with David. David was her escape from work, her escape from thinking, from constantly analyzing every single person in her life until she couldn't breathe.

He was easy. Or at least, he was supposed to be.

70

That wasn't fair to him, though. She knew that. Every adult who's ever had a relationship knows that they take hard work to maintain. She couldn't expect to just float along.

She took another deep breath, and as she released it, she had to admit that there was more than just a desire for relaxation behind the damage to her relationship. Try as she might to escape it, there was still one thing in her life that she couldn't leave behind. The monkey was still on her back and when she allowed herself to think, it quickly became all she could think about.

She recalled her date with David the night she received this case. He had accused her of tuning him out while she brainstormed about the copycat Donkey Killer case, and he was right. She had ignored him so she could toss around the possibility that Clark was the killer.

And she still fixated on that. This case was frustrating, and difficult enough that she was able to push it to the back of her mind, but now it was in the front of her mind, and though she tried to cling to David's memory, her impatience shifted focus.

Abel had responded more consistently than David, but his responses were all a flavor of *Still working on it.*

She needed to know. She needed to know if the man she reported to every evening was a murderer. She needed to put an end to this damned case so she could move on with her life. Doctor West insisted she should just let it go, but she couldn't. She couldn't just let Trammell win.

Trammell's dead, Faith, Doctor West's voice echoed in her mind.

"Doesn't matter," she said out loud. "I need this. I need to beat this killer. Even if he's just a knockoff, I need to win."

She hung her head in her hands and squeezed her eyes shut against the hot tears that filled the corners of her eyes. She felt a soft, furry head worm its way under her arms onto her lap and looked down to see Turk staring up at her, his eyes filled with the pure compassion that only dogs could express.

She smiled and in an uncharacteristic display of affection, dropped to her knees and hugged Turk tightly. Turk leaned his head on her shoulder and let her hold him until she gained control of her breathing and the tears subsided.

She sat back on her chair and took a final deep breath. "Thank you, buddy. I feel better now."

Turk barked and Faith chuckled and ruffled his head.

71

Her phone buzzed, and she felt a rush of excitement. Could that be David?

It wasn't David. It was Abel. *Got info. Emailing file.*

Her heart began to beat rapidly. She quickly opened her laptop. As she waited for it to boot, her phone rang again. She answered and Steinholz's voice said, "Good morning, Agent?"

"Morning," Faith replied. "What do you have for me?"

"I have a drug," he said. "A surprisingly, deceptively simple drug that when interacting with carfentanil and pancuronium has a rather wonderful effect. Well, not wonderful. Terrifying and insidious, actually, but wonderful because it puts us one step closer to the end of this case."

"What is it, Steinholz?" Faith asked, struggling to remain patient.

"It is guaifenesin," he said.

He fell silent, and after a moment, Faith said, "And what is guaifenesin?"

"Guaifenesin," Steinholz explained, "is a centrally acting muscle relaxant. It is found in very small doses in cough medicine. It is found in much higher doses in sedated animals, particularly in zoos."

"Yes," Faith said, "we're heading to the National Zoo. We'll ask about guaifenesin when we arrive."

"Don't bother," Steinholz said. "The National Zoo uses Dantrolene. It has a similar effect, but it's not present in our victims. However, the Maryland Zoo in Baltimore uses guaifenesin. They also use carfentanil and pancuronium. Crucially, they never use all three or any two in conjunction. Would you like to know why?"

"Yes, that would be nice," Faith said, taking a breath to calm herself.

"Because when you use pancuronium or guaifenesin by themselves, they cause muscle relaxation. When you use either of them with carfentanil, they cause acute respiratory failure. When you use all three, something interesting happens. The guaifenesin interacts with the carfentanil causing greater adrenaline production. I'm not sure how this occurs, but it does, and it explains the elevated levels of free testosterone I found in both of our victims. It's how our victims stayed alert and alive for days before the cocktail of drugs finally shorted out their cardiovascular system."

"Guaifenesin interacts with pancuronium by causing contradictory muscle contractions and stiffness. In short, the two muscle relaxants acting together cause muscles to do the opposite of relaxation. So our

72

killer pumped a precise dosage of all three drugs to keep our subjects alive, then a precise dosage of... well, frankly any one of the three to kill them, although as nearly as I can tell, he used a massive dose of guaifenesin to induce heart failure."

"You said the Maryland Zoo?" Faith asked, grabbing her notepad and pen.

"That's one," Steinholz confirmed. "Well, there are many zoos that use these chemicals, but the Maryland Zoo is the closest."

"Wonderful," Faith said. "Thank you."

"Don't mention it, Special Agent. I am happy to help."

After Steinholz hung up, Faith looked up the address and contact number for the zoo. They would open at eight a.m. Faith intended to be there at seven to talk to management before the zoo opened to the public.

She looked at the address again and frowned. She searched her maps and found that the zoo was only a half-mile away from the coffee shop where the latest victim—still unidentified—had been taken.

She smiled as she sensed her noose tighten around their killer. "Gotcha," she whispered.

She minimized the browser and opened her email. She clicked on Abel's email, but just before she could download the attachment, the bathroom door opened. She quickly closed the email and opened the internet browser.

"Whatcha looking at?" Michael asked, approaching her.

"The Maryland Zoo," Faith said, gesturing at the screen. "A half mile away from the coffee shop where our mystery victim was grabbed, and get this: Steinholz found the third drug, and our friends at the zoo here use all three of the drugs regularly."

"What's the third drug?"

"Guaifenesin."

Michael frowned. "The stuff in cough syrup?"

"And apparently in animal-grade muscle relaxants. I guess it interacts with carfentanil and pancuronium in ways that keep victims alive and rigidly paralyzed for a little while. It also kills people who are injected with too much."

"And won't trip a tox screen because it's commonly found in cold medicine," Michael said, putting two and two together. "So our mystery guy works at the zoo, probably for the veterinary department."

"Most likely," Faith said.

"Have you called the zoo?"

"No one's going to be there yet," Faith said, "I'm thinking we go there now, and maybe we don't call ahead. Just in case our baddy is a shot-caller who could conceivably cover any tracks he may have left."

Michael grinned. "Well, looks like we have a good day ahead of us."

Faith smiled. "Fingers crossed."

Michael turned to start dressing, and while he did, Faith quickly closed her email. It grated on her nerves that she couldn't follow up on whatever information Abel had for her, but she would have to deal with it. She couldn't follow up with Michael looking over her shoulder, and they were running against the clock in this case. The email would still be there later.

Still, as they drove toward the zoo, Faith's thoughts continued to drift toward the copycat Donkey Killer case. Clark's face hovered in the back of her mind, but it brought no fear now.

I'm coming for you, Clark, she thought.

***

"I told you," the administrator insisted, jutting her jaw forward defiantly. "We don't hire criminals."

"No one's holding you responsible for this individual's actions," Faith said, "but it is very likely that unbeknownst to you, one of your employees is responsible for at least two murders and one kidnapping, possibly many more of both. You need to be forthcoming with us."

"*You* need a *warrant*," the middle-aged woman who was not nearly as mousy as she looked replied. "You can't just show up here and expect us to throw everything aside based on a coincidence!"

"Look, Mrs. Slattery," Michael said impatiently. "We can go get a warrant and in the process turn this into an official investigation into your zoo, complete with media coverage, or you can work with us, and we'll do everything we can to make sure the news doesn't get out. If it does get out, we'll make sure everyone knows how helpful you were and how critical your help was to our investigation."

Slattery looked between the two agents uncertainly, tapping her pen on her desk. Finally, she sighed and said, "Well, what do you want to know?"

"We need to know who has access to these chemicals," Faith said. "Particularly, any Caucasian male in their late twenties to early thirties who has access to them."

Slattery lifted a hand and let it drop. "Nearly our entire veterinary staff is Caucasian and male. Don't judge me for that, that's just who applied."

"How many people, Miss Slattery?"

"At least two dozen," she said.

"Any with a criminal background?"

"No!" Slattery cried. "I told you. We don't—"

"Yeah, we get it," Michael interrupted, "but mistakes happen, so we're going to run some background checks anyway."

"Go ahead," Miss Slattery said, "you won't find anything. We're very careful."

Faith and Michael commandeered the administrator's desk and plugged their laptops in. As promised, there were twenty-four people who could potentially match Ms. Hollister's description who also had access to the chemicals described. Most of these individuals were veterinary doctors, nurses, or orderlies, but a few were couriers or janitors and one was a security officer assigned to patrol the medical wing at night.

Still, they were on the right track. One of these individuals was their killer.

After three hours of very extensive background checks, however, they found no indication of a criminal background among any of the employees.

"You see?" Miss Slattery said triumphantly. "We take the safety of our guests and staff very seriously. No one with any sort of criminal background is employed at my zoo."

"I commend you on your thoroughness, Miss Slattery," Michael said, "but we still need to investigate. We need to speak with every one of these employees, today if possible."

"Well, it's not possible," she said. "Only nine of them are on shift right now."

"We'll start with them," Michael said. "Is here a good place to talk?"

Miss Slattery's lips thinned, but as frustrated as she was, she was just mature enough to understand that an active murder investigation trumped convenience. She nodded and said, "I'll set up a meeting room for you. Can you give me twenty minutes?"

"Sure," Michael said, "and thank you for your cooperation."

Slattery offered the thinnest excuse for a smile Faith had ever seen, but she followed through. Twenty minutes later, Faith and Michael

75

were in a meeting room with nine very scared employees lined up outside the door.

It took three more hours to question the employees. All nine of them present had alibis for the morning of the abduction. Six had alibis for the night Guiver and Levant were dumped, but since none of the three could have been at the coffee shop at the time of the latest kidnapping, there was no point in following up on those.

Faith wasn't exactly disheartened. They still had fifteen employees to question. She was impatient, however. It had been two days since the last abductee was taken. Time was running out for him if it hadn't already. The police department had somehow still failed to identify him, and though Faith was sure they were close to the killer, they were still too far.

Then another concern struck her. If these employees talked to their coworkers—and they surely would regardless of whatever commitment to silence they made—then the killer could be spooked. Spooked kidnappers didn't tend to keep their abductees. Sometimes they would leave them somewhere unharmed and disappear, but Faith doubted this man would leave his victim alive.

They returned to Miss Slattery's office. The administrator was irritable but less argumentative than before and agreed to provide contact information for the employees who were not present along with their work schedules.

As she printed the addresses, she gasped. Faith raised an eyebrow. "What is it?"

"I... I just remembered," she said, her voice thready and her face pale.

"What did you remember?" Michael asked.

"Oh God," she said.

She reached weakly for her chair and Michael quickly went around the desk and helped her sit. "What is it?" Michael asked. "What did you remember?"

"I... I should have thought," Miss Slattery said. "I was only thinking about current employees. It didn't occur to me that a former employee could be involved."

Faith and Michael shared a look. They hadn't thought of that possibility either.

"How could a former employee have access to these drugs?" Faith asked.

"Well, he couldn't," Miss Slattery said, "but Jeffrey Linklater was fired for negligence. Specifically, negligence as a security officer. He left the drug locker unlocked several times, and three weeks ago, we noticed drugs missing. He was fired for that."

"What drugs were missing?" Faith asked.

Slattery met her eyes. "Carfentanil," she whispered.

Faith and Michael met each other's eyes again. "Do you have his address still?"

"Um… I think so."

Slattery found the address and gave it to the agents. It was an apartment complex ten minutes from the zoo and five from the coffee shop. They stood and as they prepared to leave, Miss Slattery said, "I'm sorry. I didn't know. I didn't…"

"It's not your fault," Michael said. "Sometimes you can do everything right and still get burned. Keep your phone on. We'll be back to talk to your other employees if Mr. Linklater turns out to be a dead end."

"Okay," Miss Slattery said, clearly not enthused by the thought.

On their way to Jeffrey's apartment, Faith thought about Miss Slattery. She reminded her of a woman they had run into in Tucson. She had initially been belligerent as well, but like Miss Slattery, when it was revealed that one of her employees was indeed the killer, she had reacted with the same shell-shocked expression.

She wondered if that woman—she couldn't remember her name, Darla or Donna or something—had ever recovered from that. She wondered if Miss Slattery would ever recover.

She wondered if the boss would ever recover if Clark turned out to be the copycat Donkey Killer after all.

CHAPTER TWELVE

Clark stared at the victim in the chair and struggled to keep his bile from escaping through his mouth. He glanced at Desrouleaux and saw the same grimace of nausea on his face.

Chavez wasn't so lucky. The rookie waited outside of the room. Clark could hear her heaving from where he stood.

The woman, like most of the victims before her, had bled out from multiple shallow lacerations and several deep ones. Not one of the lacerations, even the deep ones, were fatal in and of themselves. No major blood vessels were impacted, and no major organs were damaged. The only serious injuries were severed tendons behind each knee and ankle, and in this case, severed tendons in the woman's biceps. How the killer had managed to avoid nicking the brachial artery was beyond Clark.

She looked inhuman. Many of the cuts were on her face, and her skin was covered in dried blood. You could see where her tendons had been severed in her legs and arms. Her facial expression was one of sheer terror, and Clark couldn't blame her.

Strictly speaking, Clark was supposed to allow Desrouleaux and Chavez to handle the day-to-day while he babysat Faith, but Desrouleaux had asked him to come help with this scene, and anyway, Faith was doing all right.

He shivered as he imagined Faith as the victim instead of this stranger. Faith had fallen prey to the original Donkey Killer, and only last-minute heroics by Michael Prince had saved her from a fate like this one.

Looking at the mangled body of the victim, Clark understood now why Faith obsessed so much over this case. If someone had hurt him the way that animal hurt Faith, he would be just as obsessed as she was. In fact, he would probably have gone all the way off the deep end. Frankly, it was impressive as hell that she managed to maintain any semblance of normalcy.

"Well, she was always stronger than most," Clark said.

"What's that?" Desrouleaux asked.

"Nothing," Clark said, "anything new to report evidence wise?"

"CSI grabbed the usual. Nothing identified yet. The coroner's going to perform an autopsy, but I'll bet you a donut I know what's gonna come back from that."

"Yeah," Clark said, "No mystery there. How's Chavez doing?"

Desrouleaux sighed. "Between you and me, I'll be surprised if she lasts another week."

"That bad, huh?"

Desrouleaux shrugged. "She's a smart kid, but being smart doesn't help you sleep at night after seeing something like this. This is the second body we've found in the past week, and the last one looked worse than this one."

"Jesus," Clark said, shaking his head.

"You know how it is," Desrouleaux said. "You're old hat, just like me, even if you're new to the Bureau. She's just a kid. Straight out of college. We need to start requiring five years of experience before we accept field agent candidates."

"Bold didn't have five years of experience," Clark pointed out.

"Bold is a Marine," Desrouleaux countered. "Those people eat nails for breakfast. I'll bet anything she's still pissed at Michael for shooting the first Donkey Killer before she had a chance to beat him down."

He smiled slightly, but when he saw Clark's expression, his smile faded. "Sorry. Bad joke."

"It was," Clark replied without a hint of mirth. "Even for you." He sighed. "Any reason we still need to be here?"

Desrouleaux shook his head. "No. CSI probably wants our asses out of here anyway."

They turned to leave, but as they did, Clark caught something out of the corner of his eye. "Hold on," he said.

Desrouleaux stopped and watched as Clark approached the victim. "You have gloves?" he asked Desrouleaux.

Desrouleaux produced a pair of latex gloves and a baggie. Clark accepted both and reached gingerly forward. He carefully grasped the thin fiber resting on the woman's skirt and placed it in the baggie.

"You don't want CSI to take that?" Desrouleaux asked.

"I do," Clark said, "and I want them to bump it to the front of the line."

Desrouleaux's eyes widened and Clark explained. "If this is from our killer, it could be the first piece of physical evidence he's left behind. I don't want to risk that it gets lost in the shuffle."

Desrouleaux nodded. "Well, do you mind if we get the hell out of here now? I'm about to join Chavez on the barf train."

"Actually, you should rejoin her," Clark said. "You're her partner. You should be there to help her through these things."

"I'll do my best, but like I said, she's on her way out."

"Let's not give up on her yet," Clark said. "She's a good kid. She deserves every chance she can get."

Desrouleaux, knowing that his former partner wasn't talking only about Chavez, asked, "You talking about Chavez or Bold?"

Clark looked up at him and asked, more harshly than he intended, "You have something to say about that?"

"Nothing you haven't ignored a dozen times before," Desrouleaux said. He sighed and added, "Look, I like Faith too, Gordie, but she's ruined. She never left that chair."

He pointed at the victim and Clark bristled. "Tell you what, Frank. You ever find yourself sitting in a chair like that, you can judge her. Until then, I don't want to hear it, okay?"

"Okay," Desrouleaux said, lifting his hands. "I just don't want to see you dragged down with her. It's bad enough that Prince is shooting his career in the foot. Nothing against you, but we both know that Prince would be SSA instead of you if he wasn't tarnished by his partnership."

"You need to stop listening to water cooler gossip," Clark said.

They left the room and the CSIs—who, as Desrouleaux had predicted, were quite happy to see the agents leave—quickly entered. Clark handed the baggie to the lead CSI and told her to move it to priority one.

***

At the office, Clark read the latest report from Faith. *Narrowed it down to twenty-four suspects. Maryland Zoo in Baltimore. Will update later.*

He sent back a thumbs-up, then leaned back in his chair and stared at the analog clock hanging above his door. Three o'clock. He had two hours to kill.

Realistically, he could leave whenever he wanted to, but he stuck around anyway in case the fiber came back before the day ended. He wanted this case. He wanted it badly and not just for himself.

Desrouleaux was right. Faith was torpedoing what should be the most celebrated career of any agent in the twenty-first century. For the first eight years of her tenure, she defied odds almost as a matter of course. Clark had only been at the office for the last of those eight years, but he recalled the way people talked about her. Love her or hate her, everyone viewed her as an almost superhuman investigator, a juggernaut of justice who could put Elliot Ness to shame.

Then Trammell had gotten her, and Trammell had broken her.

Not completely. Not yet. Faith was still a shockingly good agent. She still solved major cases as easily as Clark could tie his own shoe. She still had the best arrest record of any agent in the field office, among the top in the entire Bureau.

But she was cracking. Her immense willpower allowed her to function under stress that would kill most people, but that stress was taking its toll, and it all came back to this copycat killer case. Clark wasn't a psychologist, but it was plain to anyone who looked that this copycat killer was a stand-in for Trammell as far as Faith was concerned. If she could stop him, then she could get this monkey off her back.

But she couldn't stop him. The same mental block that prevented her from letting this case go prevented her from seeing this case clearly. Her kneejerk pursuit of Jared Greenwood was case in point. Greenwood wasn't even a person of interest anymore by the time Faith started after him. He had alibis for nearly every killing. The only reason Faith suspected him was his relationship to Horace Greenwood, the Weed Killer that Faith herself had brought to justice a month or so before she accosted Jared.

Clark sighed and leaned forward, steepling his fingers. He had hoped warning Faith off would stop her, but it clearly hadn't. She continued to poke around, even interviewing victims' families. Finally, he had reported her to the boss.

He had done that to protect her. The boss was already suspicious of her. He liked and admired her as much as Clark did, but it was impossible not to see the difference between the agent before Trammell and the agent after. If the boss had discovered that Faith was snooping on the case without his permission, he would have pulled her from the field until she passed a psych eval, which she wouldn't do, and once an agent had a failed psych eval on their record, that was it for them in the field. Faith could recover fully and completely and still never come within a hundred yards of anything that wasn't a desk.

So he had made the boss a deal. He had taken personal responsibility for Faith's behavior. He would be assigned as her supervisor and watch her like a hawk.

The boss, like Desrouleaux, had cautioned him against throwing his career away for anyone, regardless of how good they were at their job, but Clark had insisted. Faith wasn't just good, she was flawless. She was transcendent. She was a damned superhero. People like that deserved every chance they could get. They deserved for others to fall on their swords if necessary.

But Faith needed to get her shit together. She had managed to keep her obsession with the copycat case away from her job for a while, but her façade was cracking. She had made some unforgivable slipups in recent cases, including a potential diplomatic disaster in New York when her K9 had attacked a South African citizen and Faith, rather than following anything that even remotely resembled procedure, had decided to trust her dog's instincts and allow him to run down a man who turned out to be very innocent and very unhappy with his treatment at the hands of American law enforcement.

That K9 had nearly been killed by Trammell as well. Clark shook his head. They were a match made in Hell if there ever was one. He understood where Michael was coming from when he proposed that the two of them could help each other heal, and in his defense, it seemed to work at first; but now, Clark could see that their paranoia fed into each other.

Hell, Turk had actually lunged at Clark after the initial meeting where the boss had assigned Clark as Faith's supervisor. Clark chuckled mirthlessly. Maybe the dog thought he was the copycat killer.

He didn't like that a small corner of his brain thought that idea not so farfetched.

The door to his office opened and the boss poked his head inside. "Penny for your thoughts?"

Clark lifted an eyebrow as he stood. "You're visiting me? That's a first. Should I be concerned?"

"You should always be concerned," the boss said, walking inside and closing the door behind him. "But I'm not here to fire you yet."

"Yet," Clark repeated. "I love that you included that word."

"No one's safe in our job," the boss said, waving his hand to decline Clark's offer of whiskey. "And you're definitely not safe if you're offering your boss liquor on the job."

"So you don't want to talk about the vodka you keep in your locked filing cabinet?" Clark asked with a smile.

"Fair enough," the boss replied with a slight crack in his face that counted as a smile for him.

He sat in the chair in front of Clark's desk and Clark returned to his own chair. "So I assume you didn't come here to shoot the shit," Clark said.

"No," the boss said, "I came to follow up on Bold. You haven't given me a report yet."

"Yeah, I didn't want to keep sending 'Hey, she's okay' texts."

"'Hey, she's okay' texts are exactly what I want to hear," the boss replied.

"So you want me to text you right now, or should I just tell you again?" Clark replied, a little shortly.

"Take a breath, Clark," the boss said, calmly but sternly.

Clark took a breath and said, "All right. I just feel like it's not helping anything to breathe down her neck."

"Leaving her to her own devices didn't help," the boss countered. "Look, Clark, I fully appreciate that you feel bad for what Faith is going through, but we're not helping anyone by delaying the inevitable."

"I thought we talked about this," Clark said. "We agreed this is her last chance. So far, she's making the most of it. Let's give her the benefit of the doubt, and if she screws up again, I'll be the first one to sign her discharge papers."

"You'll be standing next to her defending your own job," the boss replied. "You took responsibility for her behavior, remember? You and I both know you won't lose your job because of her, but you'll lose any chance at a promotion. Ask me how I know."

"What, you?" Clark teased. "Come on. You're the happiest man I know. You would hate being Deputy Director."

"I'm content with my lot in life," the boss agreed, "but I've grown a lot since I chewed out Smythe. It occurs to me that all the problems in the Bureau I used to fight him for are still problems. I didn't make anything better by being noble. If I had kept my nose clean, I could be solving some of those problems from the inside."

"Well, I'm not exactly calling my boss a self-important fuckhead," Clark retorted.

"No," the boss allowed, "but being too much of a softie is just as bad as being too much of a hard ass. You know I love Faith like she's my own daughter, but she's losing it, Clark. She's one major mistake away from costing a lot of us our careers. Prince is a damned good agent too, but he's a lifer in the field now. He'll never make SAC, and Faith has a lot to do with that. You have potential to be an SAC. Hell, you're smart and you understand bureaucracy. You could be a Deputy Director one day."

"Faith could be the greatest field agent in the Bureau's history," Clark replied.

"Some would argue she already is," the boss replied, "but everything I said still stands."

"Why are you telling me this now?" Clark said. "It's too late to go back."

"I know," the boss said, "but I also know that if you need to fall on your sword for her again, you will, even if it kills you. I also know why."

Clark didn't respond. "That's old news, boss."

"Not to you," the boss replied with uncharacteristic gentleness. "You ruined your life over an obsession, and you don't want Faith to suffer the same fate. I get it. But be careful."

"Boss," Clark said, "I appreciate the warning, but I've heard it a dozen times already. I don't know how many times I can give you the same answer. Look, at the end of the day, you must still hold out hope for her, or nothing in Hell or even Heaven for that matter would keep you from sending her packing. You could fire her right now and blithely ignore my screams of protest without losing a minute of sleep, but you haven't. That tells me you still have hope for her. So let's do what we agreed. Let's give her this chance, and if she fails, then there's no more net. But she hasn't failed yet."

The boss nodded. He stood and said, "Well, I guess you have a point there. Just don't make the mistake of looking the other way if she screws up again. There's no more rope, Clark. For her or for you."

"Loud and clear, boss," Clark replied.

The boss nodded again, then left the office. Clark slumped back in his chair with a heavy sigh. He looked at his phone. No update from Faith yet.

"Come on, Bold," he said softly. "You can pull through this. Just stay strong."

CHAPTER THIRTEEN

They reached Jeffrey Linklater's apartment just after three-thirty. Faith knocked on the door while Michael and Turk positioned themselves on either side. Michael's hand crept over his handgun and the three of them steadied themselves as they waited for an answer.

There was none. After a moment, Faith called, "Jeffrey Linklater? FBI! Open up!"

There was still no answer. Faith tried again, calling louder and more forcefully. When there was still no answer, Faith looked at Turk and said, "Can you hear anything boy? Any weird smells?"

Turk trotted to the door, but after a moment, he snorted and trotted back to his place at Faith's side. Faith sighed and straightened. "He's not home. Dammit."

"Y'all looking for Jeffrey, you can find him at the Sunshine Mart," a voice said.

They turned to see Jeffrey's neighbor leaning out of her doorway.

"He works security there ever since he got fired from the zoo," the elderly woman who looked, sounded, and smelled like she was halfway through her third pack of the day told them. "Guess they don't do background checks for strip mall jobs."

"Where exactly is the Sunshine Mart?" Faith asked.

"Corner of Maine and Elm," the helpful neighbor offered.

The three of them started away. "Thank you," Faith replied.

"Anything for you to stop with that racket," the older woman groused.

Faith and Michael shared a look but said nothing as they left the building.

Maine and Elm was ten minutes away in a more rundown neighborhood of the city. The Sunshine Mart looked just like every other strip mall mini-market Faith had ever seen: dirty, poorly maintained, and seemingly on the verge of a bankruptcy that it would elude against all odds until someone finally decided to invest a few billion dollars and gentrify the city, either buying the lot out or raising rent prices to an astronomically high level.

Their suspect stood outside of the minimart wearing the bored expression that only strip mall security guards could wear. He nodded impassively at Faith and Michael, unconcerned by the clear FBI logos on their vests.

That concern came in spades when he realized the agents were coming to talk to him. His eyes widened, and when they stopped in front of him, he gulped audibly.

"Everything okay, Mr. Linklater?" Faith asked.

Jeffrey started when he heard his name. "How... how do you know my name?"

"We got it from your former boss, Miss Eva Slattery."

Jeffrey cringed and looked around nervously. He gestured for the agents to follow him, but Michael said, "Here's fine, Mr. Linklater. Why are you so nervous?"

"They don't know I was fired," he said.

"Who doesn't?"

"My bosses, okay?" Jeffrey whined. "I told them I took a break from work and moved home to take care of my great-aunt. I didn't want them to know I was fired."

"Fired because you stole heavy drugs from the zoo's medical locker, you mean?" Faith asked innocently.

He cringed again and said, "Look, agents, I'll talk, okay? I'll tell you everything I know, but not here."

"Everything okay, Jeff?" a voice called.

Faith turned to see a smiling middle-aged man approach. His expression was affable, but his eyes were calculating and they never left Linklater.

"Everything's fine, Mr. Hanson. They're here to talk to me about that stolen car that almost hit me the other day. They think it's running drugs or something."

Hanson's eyes shifted to Faith, who smiled and said, "We'll only borrow him for a few minutes, Mr. Hanson."

Hanson nodded, apparently satisfied. "All right, Jeff. Take all the time you need. I'll have Charlie cover for you."

"You're a real one, Mr. Hanson," Jeff replied, offering his boss a thumbs-up.

Hanson didn't return the gesture, and as soon as he turned around, Linklater motioned for the agents to follow him. He led them to a table in front of a nearby fast-food place and sat with a heavy sigh.

"Thank you for agreeing to talk to us, Mr. Linklater," Faith said. "I'll get straight to the point. We're investigating the murders of Barret Guiver and Janice Levant as well as the abduction of a third individual."

"Murder?" Linklater squeaked. "Oh man. Look, I really don't know anything about that."

"Really?" Michael asked. "You don't know about the massive doses of carfentanil, pancuronium, and guaifenesin that both victims died from?"

"Oh man," Linklater repeated. He wiped sweat from his brow and grimaced as though sickened by the news. Faith looked over at Turk. He regarded Linklater watchfully but didn't react threateningly. "Look," he said, "I didn't mean for anyone to get hurt. I was working a twelve-hour shift, and I just forgot to check the medical locker to make sure it was shut before I left. I had done it a couple times before and it wasn't a big deal. I didn't think about it until I got in the next morning and Eva told me the drugs were gone. Oh man. I'm so sorry."

"Yeah, I'll bet," Michael said, pulling the crime scene photos from his pocket and tossing them on the table. "So you don't recognize these individuals?"

Linklater looked at the photos and slumped with guilt, but not criminal guilt. "No," he said glumly. "Oh man. I didn't mean for anyone to die. I mean, I didn't even think that someone might poison people. The carfentanil, I thought maybe they would cut it, like they do with fentanyl. I never even thought. God, I'm so sorry."

Faith and Michael shared a look. They could tell already that Linklater was innocent, but they had to do their due diligence anyway.

"Jeffrey, I'm inclined to believe you, but I have to ask. Can you verify your whereabouts five nights ago?"

"Yeah, I was here. The Sunshine Mart's open until midnight on weekends. Hanson can verify it, but… do you have to ask him?"

"We'll pull the security camera footage," Michael replied. "I'll tell him we think the drug runners might have stopped here for supplies before they started their little road trip."

Linklater slumped again, this time with relief. "Oh, thank you, Special Agent. That means a lot to me."

"Don't mention it," Michael said dryly.

"So you didn't take any of the drugs yourself," Faith said.

"No," Linklater repeated, shaking his head emphatically. "I don't do that shit. I had a cousin overdose on heroin."

He looked at the crime scene photos and tears welled in his eyes. Miraculously, Faith felt an echo of sympathy for him.

"Can you tell me who else might have taken them?" Faith asked. "Did anyone you work with have a drug problem? Maybe they ran with the wrong crowd or just gave you a bad vibe?"

He shook his head. "No, everyone was really cool there. Even Eva was all right when she didn't have a bug up her ass. I worked nights there, so it was usually just me and the other guard."

"Who was the other guard?"

"Yeni," he said. "Cute chick. Thick, you know what I mean? Sassy. She and I hooked up for a while. I think she still works there."

Faith and Michael shared another look. Yeni might very well still work there, but she was almost certainly not a young Caucasian man with blonde hair and blue eyes. She turned back to Linklater and said, "We're going to follow up on everything you just told us, Mr. Linklater. If there's anything you should have told us that you didn't, now is the time to let it out. If we find out another way, there are going to be serious consequences for you."

"I've told you everything," he said. He glanced at the photos and tears formed in his eyes again. "I'm so sorry," he said. "I'm so sorry that they were hurt."

"It's not your fault, Jeffrey," Faith said. "Everyone makes mistakes."

Jeffrey nodded glumly. "Look, I don't know if this helps," he said, "but I know some employees liked to sneak guests in after hours. Maybe one of the guests took the drugs."

"Who?" Faith asked.

He shrugged, "I have no idea."

"I mean which employees would sneak guests in?"

"Honestly," Jeffrey replied, "everyone. Eva doesn't run as tight a ship as she likes to think."

"So it would seem," Michael said.

***

Faith's phone rang. Clark. She frowned and set her chopsticks down. "Bold," she answered.

She didn't bother leaving the table. Michael was mechanically shoving forkfuls—or rather chopsticksfuls—of chow mein into his face and staring just as mechanically at the rerun playing on the hotel room tv. Turk sat in front of the tv, his face as listless as Michael's. She could put Clark on speaker if she wanted, and they probably wouldn't hear a word they said.

"Sorry for not replying to your text," Clark said. "There was another copycat victim."

Faith's blood ran cold, and she decided to step outside after all. "Oh?" she said, trying to sound nonchalant.

"Yeah," he said, "I spent most of the day at the scene."

He sounded flat, distracted. Faith told herself that there were any number of innocent reasons why this might be the case, but of course there were less-innocent reasons as well. "Why are you telling me this?" she asked.

He sighed. "I don't know. I guess… you're right. I'm sorry. You're not supposed to be worrying about this case. Go ahead and report."

Faith took a breath and said, "Well, the employees we interviewed today were a dead end. We learned from the zoo's administrator that a former security guard was fired for leaving the medical locker unlocked. A lot of drugs went missing when he did, including the ones our killer used."

"Have you found him yet?" he asked.

"Yes," Faith replied, "he's innocent. We verified his alibi for the night the bodies were dumped. Doesn't know who might have taken the drugs."

"Well," Clark said, "at least you know you're looking in the right place now. Good night, Faith."

"Good night," she said. Just before she hung up, she asked, "Clark?"

"Yeah?"

"Are you all right?"

There was a brief pause before Clark replied. "Yeah. I'm just tired."

Faith nodded. "All right. Talk to you later."

"Later."

She hung up and returned to her dinner. Michael had finished his and was taking his shoes off. "I'm going to turn in," he said. "We can start on the rest of the employees tomorrow. If it's not them—"

"Let's leave that consideration for later," Faith said. "I don't want to succumb to defeatism."

Michael nodded. "Fair enough. Goodnight, Faith."

Faith finished her dinner and waited until Michael and Turk were both asleep. She kept the tv on so the background noise would mask her movements, then opened her laptop and downloaded the file Abel sent her.

When she scanned it, a flurry of emotions ran through her. First, was sharp frustration and disappointment. Once more, she had wasted her time on a useless lead. Clark wasn't the killer. This file proved that Faith's suspicions were catastrophically misguided. His secretive past was clearly explained here.

The second emotion was a nearly as sharp wave of guilt. Clark had her back with the boss. By the boss's own admission, Clark was the only reason Faith still had a job, and she had thought he could be not only a serial killer but the copycat of the man who had hurt her.

The third emotion was relief. She couldn't admit it to herself while she suspected him of murder, but she actually liked Clark. He was a good agent, even if he was a little by-the-book. And he believed in Faith. That kind of support was in short supply these days.

She would need to have a long conversation with Doctor West when she returned home. She could see more clearly now how adversely this case was affecting her. She had suspected an innocent man of the worst possible sort of crime on nothing more than the strength of her dog's intuition.

A second wave of guilt, nearly as powerful as the first, coursed through her when she thought about Ellie. Who was she to judge the poor woman? Faith had never been married. She had never been divorced. She had never bound her entire life to someone else and been forced to sever that life. Where did she get off deciding that because Ellie didn't drop her ex like a bad habit that she was somehow an evil, manipulative jerk?

Because Turk didn't like her. That was why.

Faith glanced over at Turk, who slept soundly next to the bed. He was a good dog. Hell, he was the best damned dog that had ever lived. He was loyal, smart, strong, compassionate, and despite everything, he still had incredible instincts.

But not flawless instincts. He was a dog. Sometimes, he just didn't like certain people. That didn't mean those people were serial killers.

She heaved a deep sigh and read the file again, more thoroughly this time.

Supervisory Special Agent Gordon Clark had graduated from Concordia University in 2005 as Kris Hennessy. He had joined the Los Angeles Police Department in 2006, and worked his way up to the rank of Detective Sergeant within five years. In 2011, he had infiltrated the

Paisanos Locos gang. While undercover, he had earned the favor of the street boss of the Locos and through that connection, he became familiar with several high-ranking members of the Sinaloa Cartel.

His bosses tried to pull him out, but he ignored them and went deep. He tried to bring down the entire Sinaloa Cartel from within. He didn't succeed, but he did destroy the Paisanos Locos and his actions exposed several captains in the cartel and forced them into hiding. A supplementary DEA report estimated he had decreased the cartel's footprint in the United States by seventeen percent.

He was a hero.

Of course, that meant he had a price on his head. He went into witness protection in 2014 and by the time he got out in 2019, he had a new face and a new name. His family had not seen him since he entered the program, and they never would.

He had sacrificed his entire life to stop the most dangerous criminal organization in the world, and in the process, he had wounded them more than the entire DEA had done in decades. He was a hero and Faith had treated him like a murderer.

Faith sent Abel a thank-you message and promised to talk soon. Then she closed her laptop and lay awake on her bed.

She would have to let the copycat case go. It was impacting her too much and now her behavior was risking too many others. She would talk to Doctor West when she returned. She had no idea how to overcome this fixation, but she had to.

She would have to apologize to Clark as well. He didn't deserve the way she had treated him. Far from it.

She closed her eyes, and when sleep came, the nightmares didn't come with it. Faith had suffered enough for one day.

CHAPTER FOURTEEN

He looked around the table at his family and smiled. He was so grateful for all of them. Not everyone was lucky enough to have their family to support them the way his did. He decided to let them know.

"You know," he said, "I don't tell you guys enough how much I love you. Dad, you're a tough old son of a bitch, but you're the strongest man I know. I learned so much from you. If I didn't have your voice in the back of my head telling me to rub some dirt on the scrapes and keep going, then I'd be a goner by now for sure. And Mom, you've always been so supportive of me. Even when I was in my 'emo' phase, you never gave up on me."

He turned to his siblings, who regarded him with open-mouthed shock. He chuckled and said, "Yeah, I know. Who would have ever thought I would be the one to admit how much you all mean to me?" He chuckled again and said, "I remember you two used to joke to yourself that if the house ever burned down around you, the cops should look for me first."

A searing pain shot through his head. He gasped and dropped to his knees, pressing his palms to his temples. Images of charred, blackened bodies came to his mind, their flesh bubbling and popping under a rippling, seething flame. He released a low, keening sound and slammed his hands against his temple, mouthing softly at first but with increasing volume, "Bad boy, bad boy, bad boy! *Bad boy!*"

He released a hoarse cry and stood, grabbing the glass of water next to his plate and downing it in one gulp. He gasped and released another hoarse cry as he stared wildly around at his family.

"They're all here," he said, "all here. That's Dad, there's Mom, that's Dave and that's Alyssa. Everyone's here."

The pressure in his temples slowly subsided. He took a deep, shuddering breath and released it in a whoosh. He smiled shakily and said, "Sorry about that, guys. Bit of a stressful day. I forgot about work after I picked up Dad, and I had to call in sick."

A fly drifted lazily over the table. It landed on Mom's face and crawled toward her eye. When it reached her eyelashes, her eyelids spasmed and the fly took off.

"Sorry about that, Mom," he said sheepishly. "He must have come inside when I brought Dad home. I'll do a deep clean tomorrow and get everything ship-shape."

The fly buzzed lazily and landed directly on Dave's eyeball. He could see the little creature moving around on the orb. It paused next to the pupil and leaned forward until it was halfway inside. After a moment, it pulled itself out and flew off.

The other three family members struggled to turn their eyes to look at Dave. He sighed. "Don't worry about him," he said. "I'll take him out for some fresh air tomorrow. Won't that be fun, Dave? A little sunshine? You have been looking rather pale lately."

The lizard in his brain spoke up. It told him that "Dave" had died three days ago, and it was the smell and not the fly that truly alerted him. He just hadn't wanted to admit it.

Well, I'm tired! He pouted at the lizard. *I don't want to catch someone else.*

That's up to you, the lizard said, *but you need to get the body out of your house before the neighbors can smell him too.*

He sighed and stood. He had already said he'd take care of Dave, hadn't he? He would take care of him. He would find someone else, and he would have a family again.

They're not your family.

Shut up!

He walked behind Dave. When he drew close, the smell assaulted him, and he nearly gagged. He was right. He *did* need to be more proactive about dead bodies.

He drew a deep breath, shuddering once more at the odor, and reached under Dave's armpits to pick him up.

The doorbell rang, and he cried out, dropping Dave. Dave fell heavily backwards, knocking him to the floor. For a horrific moment, Dave's face turned so his empty, staring eyes met his own. He released a choked cry and scrambled out from under Dave, then to his feet.

"Fuck!" he cried out.

The doorbell rang again. "Kenny? Are you okay? What's going on?"

"I'm fine!" he called back. "I'll be there in a minute."

He swore under his breath and rushed to Dad. "Sorry, Dad," he said, grunting as he hoisted the old man over his shoulders. "I didn't know we'd have a visitor."

He carried Dad into the bedroom and dumped him onto the bed, then came back for his mother. When he went for his sister, the doorbell rang again. "Kenny?"

"Just a second!" he called.

He returned to the kitchen and stifling his revulsion, picked Dave up. When he threw him over his shoulder, the body released a sigh as the gases that were bloating him escaped. He gagged but managed to keep from throwing up. He tossed the body onto the bed on top of the others. They stared at him with bulging eyes, and he whispered. "Sorry. Just for a few minutes, okay?" then went to answer the door.

It was Bob, his supervisor from work.

"Hey, Kenny," Bob said. "How are you feeling?"

He stared blankly at Bob for a moment. Then he remembered. "Oh, right," he said, "Um, still sick."

"You too?" Bob asked.

"What?"

"Well, I was checking to see how your dad was doing. I know you two are close, and… well, you know what I went through with my dad last summer, so I just wanted to see how you were holding up."

"Oh, yeah," he said, chuckling. "Yeah, Dad's fine. He just had some chest pains. The doctor gave him some aspirin and told him to stop trying to do the yardwork on his own. You know Dad, though. He's not going to sit still."

"Oh," Bob said, "but you're sick too? What did you catch?"

He blinked and said, "Uh, flu. Yeah, flu. Real bad."

"Got it," Bob said, "Well, I brought some soup, so that will help."

He looked down and noticed the bowl in Bob's hand for the first time. Soup? Seriously? What, was Bob sweet on him? He didn't have time for this right now!

"Oh!" he said, smiling. "Thank you. That's really nice of you."

"Don't mention it," Bob said. He frowned and said, "God. Can you *smell* that?"

"N—" he begin before a draft blew from inside the house and he definitely could smell it. The odor was so strong it prompted a massive coughing fit. Bob, suddenly remembering that the flu was highly contagious, took a few steps backward.

"Well," Bob said when the coughing fit had subsided, "I can tell you need your rest. I'll leave you to it." Bob offered a wary smile, then headed out.

The lizard in his brain watched Bob carefully as he walked away. Could he suspect something or was this just a normal reaction to illness?

Bob reached his car and turned around. He smiled and waved at him, and Bob returned the smile and the wave, much more relaxed now that there was distance between him and the germs.

He was okay. Bob didn't suspect anything.

He walked inside and breathed a sigh of relief. "Too close," he muttered. "Too close."

He set the soup on the table and thought for a moment. He should bring the others back to the table so they could enjoy some soup before it got cold. He could take care of Dave tonight after everyone went to bed. As far as finding the next Dave... well, he would find someone when the time was right. He needed to stop shoehorning things to make them fit.

Having a family wasn't easy. It took sacrifice.

He stared at the soup sitting on the table and drew in a deep breath. When he exhaled, his smile returned. "Guys? That was Bob!" he called. "He brought soup!"

CHAPTER FIFTEEN

"How long do you think this will take?"

"As long as it takes, Miss Slattery."

Eva Slattery, zoo administrator extraordinaire, had rapidly recovered from the guilt she felt the day before. Since Jeffrey Linklater, security patrolman not-so-extraordinaire, turned out not to be guilty of either theft or murder, Eva was back to her imperious ways, and it took a great deal of Faith's willpower to keep from snapping at the woman.

Slattery sighed exaggeratedly and said, "Special Agent, I understand the sense of urgency surrounding this case, but I also have a zoo to run, and I can't keep interrupting my employees' workday to answer the same questions over and over."

"Well," Faith said, "these are different employees from yesterday, and we need to question every individual who fits our profile. As far as your zoo goes, I assure you that it will be better if no more people die as a result of overdose on drugs stolen from your medical locker. At the moment, there is an elderly man whose life is in grave danger from those very drugs, and the faster we can find the kidnapper, the more likely it is we can avoid a headline that reads, THIRD VICTIM DEAD FROM STOLEN ZOO DRUGS."

Miss Slattery opened her mouth to protest, but then simply said, "One of the employees is on vacation. The other two are out sick. I'll get you their contact information, although for legal purposes, I have to point out that it is against zoo policy to provide personal contact information to law enforcement without a warrant. I will be making an exception."

She left the room and Michael turned to Faith. "How kind of her to make an exception for us." He pushed a cup of coffee her way. "Here, try some zoo coffee. It's shitty."

"Thank you, Michael," Faith said drily.

Their first interviewee walked in, a nervous-looking boy of about twenty who looked like he might weigh one-fifty with a gallon of milk under each arm.

Faith smiled perfunctorily and the boy relaxed slightly. Turk barked a friendly greeting and trotted over to him, tail wagging. He sat next to the boy and presented his head for scratches, which the interviewee promptly provided, relaxing further. "Cool dog," he said.

"He's all right," Faith agreed. "I'm Special Agent Faith Bold and this is my partner, Special Agent Michael Prince. Do you consent to recording this conversation?"

The day wore on, and Faith and Michael ruled out one suspect after another. As they approached their last three interviews, Faith decided that one of the employees who called out sick must be the killer. They would wrap these three interviews up, but unless they got really lucky, Faith expected that they would find their perpetrator at home.

Or more likely having fled the city, knowing that the FBI was on their trail.

Well, that was all right as long as he left his victims behind. If they could get medical attention to the survivors along with a confirmation of who their suspect was, they could start a nationwide manhunt and then the best their killer could hope for was to make a life for himself in some other country and never return to the United States. It wasn't a perfect solution, but at this point, Faith would take any solution that kept anyone else from getting hurt.

Their third-to-last interview was at a baseball game the day of the first two murders, "Watching the Nationals get their asses handed to them as usual," and at work—verified by security footage—during the day of the most recent abduction.

Faith and Michael shared a look after he left. "Eleventh time's the charm?" Faith offered.

Michael didn't dignify that with a reply.

Then they struck gold. The moment their interviewee walked in, Turk leapt to his feet and jumped in front of Faith. He barked and growled loudly at the employee, teeth bared and ears flat on his back.

The man jumped backward and pressed himself to the corner of the wall. "What's wrong?" he asked in a high-pitched squeal. "Is he going to hurt me?"

Faith and Michael looked at each other, then back at the suspect. "That depends on you, Mr. ..."

"Hunter," he said. "Robert Hunter. My friends call me Bob."

"Well, we're friends, aren't we, Bob?" Michael said. "What say you and I go have a conversation somewhere a little more private?"

Bob looked back at Turk, who bared his teeth again and stared at him with deadly eyes. Any protest he might have lodged died before reaching his lips. He swallowed and nodded at Michael.

Faith hoped that this wouldn't turn out to be another false lead, but she remembered the last time they trusted one of Turk's hunches blindly. Needless to say, that didn't go well.

Still, just because this lead might not pan out didn't mean the next one wouldn't.

***

Michael smiled at Bob as the two agents entered the interrogation room. Faith wore a stony expression. Bob looked around wildly for Turk, relaxing visibly when he saw the dog wasn't with them.

"He's waiting outside," Faith said. "Unless you think having him here will help you talk better."

Bob's eyes widened. He shook his head rapidly from side to side.

"Suit yourself," Faith said.

She took the seat across from Bob and began, "Bob, do you consent to this conversation being recorded?"

"Umm... Do... do I need a lawyer?"

"Well, Bob, I'll be honest," she said. "It doesn't look good for you. Now, if you're absolutely confident that what you're about to tell me is going to convince me that you're not the murderer responsible for the deaths of Barret Guiver and Janice Levant and the abduction of a third gentleman from the Morning Glory Café, then you don't need to worry about a lawyer. On the other hand, if you have any doubt that you can convince me you're not a serial killer, then yes, you need a lawyer. A good one."

Bob considered her words, then put together a feeble attempt at looking defiant. "I'll talk," he said. "I don't need a lawyer."

We'll see, Faith thought. Out loud, she said, "Wonderful. Now, Bob, do you consent to this conversation being recorded?"

Bob nodded. "Sure."

She pressed the record button. "Let the record show that Robert Hunter has agreed to being recorded. Mr. Hunter, will you please state your full name for the record?"

"Robert Hunter."

She verified his birthdate and address, then asked, "Do you consent to having your place searched?"

He frowned and said, "I mean, are they gonna tear the place up?"

"I'm sure the police will do their best to leave your property undamaged," Faith said.

98

"Umm, all right then. Yes."

"Perfect."

Faith looked at Michael, who collected Bob's housekeys and stepped outside to hand them to the waiting Detectives Mickel and Harris. It wasn't especially likely that he kept his victims in his residence, but it was certainly possible; and even if they didn't find the victims, they might find evidence of the poisons or clues that could tell them where the victims were.

All assuming Bob wasn't forthcoming. Turk could scare him into compliance if it came to that, but if he somehow managed to choke down his fear of the dog, then evidence found at his apartment could be the difference between life and death.

"Okay, Bob," Faith said when Michael returned to the room, "how long have you been employed at the Maryland Zoo?"

"Um, six years," he said.

"And what is your job title?"

"Um, maintenance supervisor."

"Repairman?"

"Yeah. I mean, technically I oversee all the maintenance workers, but mostly I just write schedules and when I'm not writing schedules, I'm fixing stuff with everyone else."

"Right," Faith said. "And do you ever have access to the medical locker?"

"Um," he said, "I have to work on the plumbing in the medical facilities sometimes. I don't have a key to the medical locker, but they keep it unlocked all the time."

Faith and Michael shared a look. Faith was beginning to think that Jeffrey Linklater wasn't the only substandard security officer the zoo employed.

"How do you know they kept it unlocked?" Michael asked.

Bob shrugged. "I opened it once or twice."

Faith lifted an eyebrow. "Why?"

"Dunno. I was curious, I guess."

"I see," Faith said, "about what?"

He shrugged. "I don't know. I just... was curious."

"You're gonna have to do better than that, Bob."

He sighed and said, "Well. I just wanted to know what kind of drugs they had. I don't do drugs. I mean, I never have, but... I don't know. I was curious. I thought maybe if they had some morphine or something..." his voice trailed off.

"To be clear, Bob," Faith said, "you planned to steal morphine from the medial locker for recreational purposes?"

Bob nodded miserably, but quickly added, "I didn't steal anything, though. They didn't have anything I wanted."

"You didn't want carfentanil?" Faith asked, watching Bob's face carefully.

He showed no guilt or alarm. He shook his head and said, "No, that stuff's strong. They use that to put elephants under. Like, a milligram of that is enough to stop someone's heart."

"How do you know that?" Michael asked.

"I don't," he said.

"Then why did you say that?" Faith prompted.

"I don't know! I mean, I know it's deadly, but I don't know how much. I just guessed a milligram because it's the smallest amount I could think of. The point is carfentanil is too strong. I didn't want to risk overdosing on that."

"How many times did you open the medical locker?" Faith asked.

"Just twice," Bob said. "I kind of got over the desire to do drugs. Too much risk."

"I agree with you there, Bob. When was the last time you opened the locker?"

He hesitated and Faith said, "We're going to find out anyway, Bob. The best thing you can do for yourself right now is to be honest."

He sighed and said, "Ten days ago."

Faith and Michael shared another look. Ten days ago was four days before Barret Guiver's and Janice Levant's bodies were found. That fit perfectly with their timeline for the abductions and murders.

The third victim had been missing for four days. Faith's lips thinned, and she asked, "Why did you get into the medical locker again if you're over your desire for hard drugs?"

"Well, I'm over it now," he said. "I just... was curious."

"Bob, you need to stop saying you were just curious. See, I would believe you were curious if you just opened the locker once, but opening it again? That makes me think there's more than just curiosity going on here. You need to stop hiding things from me and just tell me the truth. Frankly Bob, at this point, lawyer or no lawyer, we're going to learn the truth anyway. How hard things are for you after depends on how easy you make things for us. You understand?"

He gulped and nodded. "Wonderful," Faith said. "So, let's try again. You opened the locker ten days ago because?"

He took a breath, "Because I wanted to see if they had morphine yet."

Faith sighed exasperatedly. "Did you take anything from the medical locker?"

"No," he said, shaking his head vigorously. "I promise!"

"What about three weeks ago?" Michael asked. "Was that you in the medical locker three weeks ago?"

"You mean when Jeffrey got fired? No, that wasn't me."

"Do you know who it was?"

"No," he said, shaking his head. "I thought it was Tommy, but he was out of town."

"By Tommy, you mean Thomas Cantrill?"

"Yeah. He's into drugs. He sells sometimes. Not all the time, but sometimes. I thought maybe he was trying to sell some stuff on the black market."

"Did you approach anyone with this information?"

"No," Bob said. "I mean, I didn't see him take it. I just thought if it were anyone, it would be him. But he was out of town anyway, so it wasn't him."

"Right," Faith said, making a mental note to follow up on Thomas Cantrill's whereabouts three weeks ago, just in case. "What are the officers going to find at your home, Bob?"

He blinked. "What?"

"You heard me."

"Yeah, I heard you, but I don't know what you mean."

Faith leaned forward, her eyes boring into Bob's. He shrank back at her gaze and swallowed.

"Stupid looks real bad on you, Bob," she said, her voice deceptively gentle. "Let's pretend you're not stupid for a few minutes, okay? What do you think I mean, Bob?"

He swallowed. "They're not going to find anything illegal if that's what you mean. I have weed, but it's legal in Maryland."

"I thought you said you weren't into drugs, Bob."

"Well, not hard drugs. Just weed."

"Were you smoking weed when you kidnapped Barret Guiver and Janice Levant?"

"No! I didn't kidnap anyone!"

"So they came willingly?" Faith asked.

"No! I mean... I didn't bring anyone to my house!"

"Where did you bring them?"

Bob's face screwed up with anger. "Look, you can't just try to trip me up into admitting something that didn't happen! I didn't kidnap anyone! I didn't kill anyone! I smoke weed after work, and I opened the medical locker to find morphine, but when I didn't find morphine, I closed the locker. That's all. You're searching my house, so you'll see I don't have anyone there. I don't know how to prove to you that I haven't been anywhere else but work and my house, but if I need to do that, then maybe I really do need a lawyer."

"Maybe you do," Faith began.

"Faith?" Michael interrupted. "May I have a word with you?"

Faith looked at him questioningly. His face was impassive, but that was probably just for Bob's benefit. Faith stood and looked at Bob with a deadly smile. "Don't go anywhere."

CHAPTER SIXTEEN

"Faith, I don't think it's him," Michael said.

Faith blinked. "Not him? What are you talking about, Michael? You saw the way Turk reacted. I haven't seen him react that way since Tucson!"

"He reacted that way in New York with Schoenmaker," Michael said.

Faith turned away and pursed her lips. Schoenmaker was the South African national Turk had incorrectly identified as their serial killer. By allowing Turk to apprehend him without probable cause, Faith had brought herself to the boss's attention in all the worst ways, culminating in his discovery via Clark that she had been interfering with the copycat Donkey Killer case.

"Look, I don't want to get into an argument about that," Michael said. "I like Turk. I think he has great instincts, but his instincts can be fooled. He could be smelling something on our guy that belongs to the actual killer. If they work closely together, then Turk could just be smelling that and not anything having to do with Bob directly."

"That's as thin a reason to stop suspecting Bob as Turk's reaction is to suspect him in the first place."

"I know," Michael said. "I know." He sighed. "The real reason I don't suspect him is probably even thinner."

"What's that?"

"I have a hunch."

"You have a hunch."

"Yes, Faith, I have a hunch," Michael said irritably. "I get hunches too. I have a hunch that Bob is not our killer. He's not acting nervous like he's guilty of murder. He's acting nervous, but when we questioned him about the murders, he seemed like he was being honest about not knowing anything about them."

"So why is he so nervous? Faith asked.

Michael shrugged. "Best guess is he lifted some carfentanil after all and doesn't want to admit it. Or he's just terrified because Turk nearly bit his head off."

Faith bristled and started to protest that Turk was perfectly in control, but Michael lifted a hand and said, "I'm not saying that Turk actually was going to hurt him, just that it probably looked that way to Bob. I'm only pointing out that his anxiety could be explained by reasons other than being guilty."

Faith took a deep breath and released it in a sigh.

"Faith, please," Michael said. "I'm asking you to trust me."

Faith looked at Michael and the pleading in his eyes finally convinced her. Michael was a good agent, and if he felt this strongly, then Faith should give him a chance to pursue his lead. Besides, her lack of trust had landed them in trouble recently.

"All right," Faith said, "but Bob stays in custody until we rule him out completely."

"Agreed," Michael said, relaxing visibly after Faith agreed to trust him. "I'll take that deal."

"So if it's not Bob, who is it?" Faith asked.

"I think it's one of the employees who called in sick. While we interviewed the others, I ruled out the employee on vacation. His social media is full of pictures of him in South Africa dating from two weeks ago through yesterday morning. He wasn't here."

"So it's one of the two sick employees," Faith said. "Which one?"

"I don't know," Michael admitted, "but I'll bet Bob does, even if he doesn't know he knows."

Faith considered. In their last case, Turk had misidentified two suspects because he smelled a similar scent as the one that later identified their killer. It was possible that he was smelling something on Bob that came from the killer. Maybe someone he had close contact with recently.

They returned to the interrogation room. Bob looked up dejectedly, and Faith asked. "Bob, you said you've only been to work and your home in the past three weeks. Is that true?"

He nodded. "Well, the grocery store a couple of times. And the gas station. Oh, and I dropped some soup off at Kenny's house."

Faith sat up straight when she heard that. Michael pushed off the wall he was leaning on and stared intently at Bob, who shrank back at their reaction.

"Kenny?" Faith prompted.

"Yeah. He's one of my maintenance workers. He left work early four days ago because his dad had a medical scare. I brought him some soup that afternoon. For his father, I mean but it turned out his dad was fine, but he had gotten sick. So I left him the soup."

"What's Kenny's full name?" Faith asked.

Michael pulled a pen and notepad and jotted down, "Kenneth Langeveldt."

"Address?" Michael asked.

"231 Lincoln Street," Bob replied. "Why? You don't think Kenny did it, did you?"

"Do you think he did?" Faith asked.

"No," Bob said, shaking his head. "There's no way. He's such a sweet guy. Takes care of his parents. Always has nice things to say about everyone. He works really hard too. He's always covering shifts and working overtime. That's why I felt so bad when he went home with his dad. I knew it had to be an emergency if he would leave work without saying anything."

"But it wasn't an emergency, was it?" Faith asked.

Bob blinked and said, "N... no." He frowned. "But he was sick. He had a horrible coughing fit when I brought the soup."

"I see," Faith said. "Did you notice anything suspicious at his house?"

Bob shook his head. "No. I mean, I didn't go inside."

"You went to his house, but you didn't go inside?"

"No. He took the soup at the door. He was sick, and he didn't want to get me sick, so he didn't invite me inside. I figured he was just trying to be safe. Besides..." he blushed a little, "I didn't really want to go inside once I got there."

"Why not?" Faith asked.

He shook his head. "Man, it *stank* in there. When he opened the door, it was like someone opened a grave and..." His voice trailed off, and he looked at Faith in shock. "Oh God," he whispered.

***

The sun was touching the horizon when they arrived at 231 Lincoln Street. The neighborhood was a well-to-do suburb, but not excessively fancy. One of those small houses, big yards kind of neighborhoods.

Perfect if you don't want the smell of dead bodies reaching your neighbors.

The three of them got out, and the moment Turk sniffed the open air, he stared straight at the house and growled low in his throat.

"Steady, boy," Faith said softly. She radioed Mickel that they were about to approach, and Mickel replied, "Ten-four."

She and Michael drew their weapons and started up the lawn. Faith and Turk positioned themselves on either side of the doorway on the porch while Michael knocked. The sound of old-style jazz music wafted out to them.

"FBI!" he called. "Kenneth Langeveldt! Open up!"

No sound other than the radio came from inside the house.

Michael knocked again, "Kenneth Langeveldt! Open up and let us in! We can do this the easy way or the way that gets people hurt! What do you want to do?"

There was no response. Michael looked at Faith, who nodded and braced herself.

Michael lifted three fingers up and retracted one at a time. When he pulled his last finger back into a fist, he lifted his leg and kicked hard. The door splintered inward and the three of them immediately rushed into the home. Turk rushed past them, and ran through the home, barking wildly.

Faith kept one ear out for signs of a struggle or a change in Turk's cries that would indicate he had found someone as she cleared the living room. Michael headed to the bedroom and cleared it while she checked the guest bathroom.

The house was a single story, and within two minutes, they had cleared all but the dining room. Turk rushed past them, and as soon as he entered the dining room, his cries changed, becoming louder, higher-pitched, and more insistent.

Faith and Michael entered the dining room behind him, prepared for a firefight. Faith leveled her weapon at a man sitting on one side of the table. He regarded her with a horrified expression but remained perfectly still.

He was around five-foot-seven, paunchy, and white-haired. He appeared to be about sixty-five years of age and wore a corduroy sweater.

"Shit," she said, holstering her weapon and rushing to the older man's side. On the way, she glanced around the table and saw two others, a woman around the same age as their coffee shop abductee and a younger woman around Janice Levant's age. Both of them wore the same horrified expressions as the older man and both sat rigidly upright, unable to move except for their eyes, which followed Faith as she checked their pulses one by one.

106

While she did this, Michael cleared the backyard, returning just as Faith confirmed that all three victims were still alive. "Backyard's clear," Michael said. "Langeveldt isn't here." He gestured at the three victims. "Are they…"

"Alive," Faith confirmed. She radioed Mickel. "Be advised, house is clear, repeat, house is clear. No sign of Langeveldt. Three victims present, alive but in need of emergency medical attention."

"Ten-four," Mickel said. "Emergency services are on their way."

Faith put her radio away and looked at the three victims. "Don't worry," she said. "Help is on the way."

She wasn't sure if they could hear her, but the older woman blinked unsteadily and her stare seemed somewhat less horrified.

The EMTs arrived a few minutes later and quickly administered emergency antinarcotics to the victims. They relaxed enough that the EMTs were able to help them onto stretchers, but none of them were able to form any coherent speech. Faith handed her card to the EMT with strict instructions to call her as soon as the victims were able to talk. He promised to contact her, then started loading the victims into the waiting ambulances.

While the EMTs attended to the victims, the two agents and the two detectives searched the house more thoroughly. They didn't find any sign of where Langeveldt might have gone, but they found more than enough evidence to confirm him as their killer, not that the paralyzed victims weren't enough.

His dresser in his bedroom was filled with vials. One drawer was filled with carfentanil, another with pancuronium, and another with guaifenesin. A fourth was filled with single-use syringes, the kind diabetics could pick up over the counter at drugstores. There was an insulin reader and a prescription bottle of insulin as well, but the prescription was years old and filled out for a Travis Langeveldt, his actual father, Faith assumed. The batteries of the insulin reader were dead. He clearly bought the reader as a cover to explain the syringes.

Michael found a photo album filled with photos of Langeveldt's actual family. Many of the photos, were torn up or scribbled over, but many were left intact. The people in the photos bore a passing resemblance to the victims, or rather, what the victims might have looked like as adults, just enough to confirm that Langeveldt was kidnapping people to replace his family.

The pictures stopped abruptly eighteen years ago. The last entry in the photo album was a newspaper clipping of an article from the time that read FOUR DEAD IN HOUSE FIRE. Scribbled underneath the headline was "Not true! I saved them!!"

Faith looked grimly at Michael. She would bet anything that the fire was no accident.

A moment later, her deduction was confirmed when Mickel called them to the garage and showed them a stack of dozens of bottles of lighter fluid, several gas cans—mostly empty but a few full—and a pile of lighters and matches.

"Got a pyro on our hands," Mickel said.

"A reformed pyro, anyway," James agreed. "Sick fuck."

"So?" Michael asked. "What do we do now?"

Faith glanced at the rubber tracks that led out of the garage. She stooped and scraped at the freshest-looking layer. It smudged easily.

She stood and said, "We wait here. He's coming back."

Mickel nodded. "All right. I'll move our vehicle. The EMTs should be out in a few minutes."

"Hey!" one of the EMTs called. "I think the killer just got here!"

The four investigators shared a look then sprinted out of the garage. They drew their weapons and met the visibly shaken EMT on the porch. He pointed toward the forested hills behind the house. "He's going there."

Faith looked up just in time to see a flash of blonde hair before it disappeared into the trees.

"Turk!" she called. "After him!"

The dog took off with a growl and the four officers sprinted after him.

Faith felt her blood rise in the familiar way as she followed Turk into the forest.

It's over, Langeveldt, she thought. *We've got you.*

CHAPTER SEVENTEEN

He was uncharacteristically quiet on the way home. He was always quiet when he had to dump his brother's body.

None of them were particularly kind to him, but Dave was the worst. Mom could be bitingly sarcastic, but Dave was sadistic. He was so happy whenever his words caused Kenny to cry.

"See? I said you were a crybaby!"

The voice was so clear that he shrieked and looked wildly around, expecting his brother to be in the back seat, grinning his evil grin like he always did.

That's your own voice, the lizard in his brain said. *Watch the road.*

He turned back to his driving just in time to swerve out of the way of an oncoming semi. He laughed nervously at the near miss. "Wow!" he said, grinning. "That was a close one."

"Would have served you right, crybaby," Dave's voice said.

"Fuck you," he muttered. He grinned and said, "I might be a crybaby, but you're a roasted sausage!"

He laughed uproariously at the joke, but when the image of his brother's blackened, shriveled body came to his mind, he choked his laughter off and turned the radio on. It played that old song about having a pocketful of sunshine. His lips turned down as he recalled his sister walking into his room while he played that song.

"Really?" she had said. "God, that song's for babies!"

She had laughed then, that ugly titter that reminded him of a cross between a witch's cackle and the mocking giggles the girls at school used to give him. At least until he hit his growth spurt. Then the girls couldn't get enough of him, could they? All of a sudden, they were desperate for some attention from Kenny Langeveldt.

He smiled again, a triumphant sneer, and said, "That's what you get, Mom. You always said no one would ever love me. Well, a lot of girls loved me. They loved me a lot. Carly cried when I broke up with her, did you know that? She said no one could ever satisfy her the way I did."

He thought of his father, and his smile disappeared as his lips curled up in rage.

Dad never teased him the way the others did. He never insulted him or laughed at him. He never did much of anything to him. Never held him, never touched him, never smiled at him. Never said he was proud of him or so happy to have him as a son. No, that was all reserved for Dave. Dave, who broke into Dad's liquor cabinet when Kenny was thirteen and force-fed him so much vodka that he had to go to the hospital. Dave, who when Kenny brought Angie Carpenter home to study with him, had sneaked into Kenny's room and held a pillow over his face until he passed out. Angie never talked to him after that, but Dad didn't have a problem with that, did he? No because Dave was the golden child, the good son, the one who made him proud. Dave, who had once told Kenny that when Kenny finally killed himself, he would frame his suicide note and tack it above his bed.

"Well, how did that work out, Dave?" he said, but it was the lizard's voice that came out, and not his own. "Who's dead now? Oh. Why that would be you. And you, Alyssa. And you, Mom. And you, you pathetic, sorry excuse for a dad. You're all dead, and I'm alive, and if you get to be alive, it's only because I say so. Now you all listen. Now you're all kind to me. Now you all are under my control. How does that feel, Dave? Do you like them apples? Fucking prick."

He grinned at the epithet. Mom always beat him when he swore, but Mom wasn't there to beat him anymore, was she?

No sir. Mom was dust, six feet underneath the Rosewood Memorial Cemetery, just like the others. Except when he kept them home to play for a while in their doppelgangers' bodies.

He recalled the first time he had found a doppelganger. He didn't really believe in doppelgangers or spirits or ghosts or anything like that. The psychologist had assured him that it was only his imagination that caused him to fear that his family would return. She had also said that it was his grief that made it difficult to let them go. She was wrong about that, but that was okay. She couldn't be expected to know.

He had moved on well enough. The spirits were quiet, and no ghosts came to plague him at night. He began to believe that the past was behind him, and he could live a normal life, just like anyone else.

Then he had seen Dave at work one day. He was repairing a broken ticket machine when he looked up and there he was, chatting with Angie Carpenter.

He knew it was Angie because she had a little birthmark under her ear. She didn't recognize him, but that was all right. He had moved on from her and anyway, she was a victim of Dave's abuse just like he was. It wasn't her fault.

But there she was, an adult now, and instead of being angry with Dave, she was smiling and flirting with him, like it was the most wonderful thing in the world that he was there with her. He stared at them, his heart beating quickly, and when Dave looked his way, he nearly collapsed with fear.

But it wasn't Dave. Of course it wasn't. It was just his doppelganger, a sliver of his spirit inhabiting a new body. The sliver didn't recognize him and after nodding politely turned his attention back to Angie Carpenter.

He had broken into the medical locker that night and stolen enough drugs to take Dave and kill him a hundred times. He didn't really think about it at first, but after he brought Dave home, he realized. He needed all of them. He could take all of them. He could finally have a family, a real family, one that loved and supported him. One that *listened* to him, that valued what he had to say.

The lizard in his brain was born at that moment. It commented viciously that at the very least, they would keep their mouths shut.

He let the lizard run the show mostly. The lizard was smart. It was cold and calculating. Most importantly, it was calm and thought quickly on its feet, like it had at the coffee shop with Dad.

Dad wasn't going to last much longer. Already his heartbeat was irregular. His mom and sister would make it another few days but Dad probably had one night left in him before he was a goner too. He would have to find Dave quickly so he didn't have two people missing at once.

He turned the corner to his house, humming a tune, once again calm now that Dave and his memory were safely dumped in the trash compactor behind the Sunny Hills Mall. He looked toward his house and slammed on the brakes. A low keening whine escaped his lips as he stared ahead.

They had found him.

They had caught him.

They had finally got to him.

He began to breathe rapidly, heart pounding, as he saw the police cruiser and the three ambulances. There was a fourth vehicle there, an unmarked SUV with tinted windows. They must have been surveilling him. They must have seen him bring Dad home.

Dad!

He watched in horror as Dad was wheeled out on a stretcher. From this distance, he could just make out Dad's arm as it lifted slightly from the stretcher until one of the EMTs grabbed his hand.

Oh no. Oh God no.

He made another soft keening noise as Mom and Alyssa followed Dad out of the house.

It was over.

One of the EMTs looked up and met his eyes. He paused a moment, staring quizzically at his stopped car. Then his eyes widened. He cried out and rushed back to the house.

Move! The lizard commanded. *Now!*

He slammed on the gas and turned the wheel. The tires screamed as the car struggled to accelerate and veer left at the same time. A few seconds later, the tires grabbed hold and the vehicle launched forward. It hopped the curb with a sickening jolt and proceeded up the short hill toward the forest. He slammed on the brakes and the car skidded to a halt a few yards from the trees.

He could get to the cave. He would be okay. He could get to the cave and hide out. He had prepared for this. The lizard had warned him that one day, he would be caught. He couldn't expect to kidnap people indefinitely. They were going to find him one day, and when that day came, he would need to hide until things calmed down, then travel to Canada. He had cash and a fake ID he could use. He would head to Canada and live a normal, law-abiding life. He would be okay.

Then he heard the dog.

He released another keening wail but cut it off when the lizard reminded him that the dog could hear him as well as smell him.

Well, he could deal with that.

He veered left and sprinted through the thickening brush. He moved effortlessly through the scrub, having familiarized himself completely with the area in case he had to escape exactly as he had to now. Behind him, he could hear the dog's calls grow louder.

He didn't have much time.

He reached the creek and jumped feet first into it. The water only came up to his waist, so he dropped down and rolled around until he was soaked. He remembered his phone then and ripped it from his pocket, tossing it into the river. He didn't need it right now.

He jumped out of the creek and sprinted ahead on the opposite bank, ignoring the stitch that began to form in his side. He huffed and puffed and grimaced but forced himself forward. When he heard the dog's cries grow fainter behind him, he crossed the creek again and continued toward the cave at a more manageable pace.

Still, he didn't stop until he reached the cave. It wasn't much of a cave, more of a hollowed-out space in the dirt supported by a network of roots over his head, but that was all right. He had a sleeping bag, some rations—water and energy bars—and crucially now that his clothes were soaked, a change of outfit.

His bag was here too, and with it five thousand dollars in cash and a wallet and passport with his Canadian ID under the name of Roman Kowalski.

"Roman Kowalski," he repeated.

The name came easily to his lips. That was good. He would be okay.

He changed out of his wet clothes then settled against the wall of the cave and closed his eyes. He steadied his breathing, and when his heart rate slowed, he ate one of the energy bars and drank some water.

He would be okay. They wouldn't find him here.

CHAPTER EIGHTEEN

This was turning out to be a disaster.

Faith stood on the bank of the creek that Langeveldt had crossed. Turk wandered around the edge of the bank, occasionally barking, and running a few yards up and down, but not retracing the scent. When they first lost Langeveldt, Faith carried Turk across the water, but the scent had been dulled enough by the river that Turk was unable to pick it up.

So now, they were making their way slowly up the river in the direction Langeveldt had been heading before they lost him. Mickel and James were coordinating police efforts including a half-dozen K9s whose cries could occasionally be heard through the forest as they searched for the elusive murderer. The forest service was watching every entrance and exit to the forest and the police were surrounding every paved road, so Langeveldt was effectively cut off from escape, but cut off from escape still allowed him hundreds of thousands of acres of forest to travel through, and if he had even the most basic survival skills, he could last for days without needing to find civilization, longer than the police and forest service could afford to patrol. If he had a cache of supplies, and Faith was certain he did, then that could stretch into weeks or even months.

Her phone buzzed. Clark. *Washington F.O. is deploying agents to widen the net. If he slips past the police cordon, we'll get him. Stay calm and stay strong.*

Faith would have bristled at the rookie advice under other circumstances, but since she *was* on the verge of losing her cool, she appreciated the encouragement. Besides, she didn't have any room to be angry at Clark considering she had spent the last several weeks suspecting him of serial murder.

She texted back. *Will do. K9s tracking. Will update later.*

"He's got to be nearby," Michael said. "He was running hard. He won't have the stamina to make it more than a few miles from his house."

"The larger issue is that he might still be moving."

"Well, that's what the K9s are for. It's not just the nose, it's the ears. They'll be able to hear him moving. He's not going anywhere."

Faith nodded. She knew that in all likelihood, Michael was right, but that did little to lessen her frustration at his escape. She had never lost a suspect like this before. Turk had never lost a suspect like this before.

Well, it may not have ever happened to Faith before, but it had happened. That's why they had procedures like this.

Still, it grated on Faith. She radioed Mickel. "Any updates?"

"Nothing yet," Mickel replied. "We're pretty confident he's still in the forest, but other than that, we don't know."

"Any chance you have tracking experts?" Faith asked. "Humans, I mean? Anyone who could track footprints and torn undergrowth or anything like that?"

"God, I wish," Mickel replied. "If it comes to that, I'm sure the National Guard will contribute some experts, but right now, it's just us and the dogs."

Faith nodded. "Yeah, I figured. Just grasping at straws."

"Grasp away. You never know which straw will lead to a rope."

Turk barked suddenly. He barked again and ran back to Faith.

"Hold on," Faith said, "Turk's got something."

Once Turk had Faith's attention, he sprinted ahead, following the river but angling off a few degrees to the north.

Jackpot.

"Mickel, Turk has the scent," Faith radioed. "Michael and I are inbound following Turk."

"Hot dog," Mickel replied. "No pun intended. Let us know when you find the bastard."

"Will do."

Faith replaced the radio in its clip and picked up the pace. Turk, far more agile than any eight-year-old German Shepherd had a right to be, leapt over branches and slid under roots, hopping through the uneven ground, and effortlessly avoiding every obstacle in his path. Faith picked up her pace even further, but she struggled to keep up with the dog. Michael huffed and puffed just behind her but managed to keep up in spite of his greater bulk.

"Come on, Turk," she whispered. "Come on."

They made it about a half-mile before the terrain got even rougher. Thick branches and heavy undergrowth impeded them and Faith had to high step to keep from tripping. She marveled that Langeveldt could make it through this for any kind of distance.

Her foot came down on a root and caught underneath it. She fell heavily forward. Her ankle wrenched underneath her, and she felt a soft pop.

She cried out and grimaced as pain shot through her like electricity. An uncomfortable spasm coursed through her other ankle and both of her knees as her mind recalled the feeling of Jethro Trammell slicing her tendons open.

"Faith!" Michael cried, sliding to a stop near her.

Turk, hearing the commotion, skidded to a halt and ran back to Faith, barking with alarm.

"I'll be fine," she said, carefully extracting her ankle. "Go get Langeveldt."

"We can't leave you here," Michael said. "He could find you like this and hurt you."

"I'll call for help," Faith promised, "and unless Langeveldt's bulletproof, he'll be in for a shock if he tries to hurt me."

Michael hesitated and he and Faith shared a charmingly concerned look. "I'll be fine," Faith repeated. "I promise. Go get him, Michael. Please."

Michael sighed and nodded. "Come on, Turk," he said.

Turk lingered, whining, and staring at Faith.

"Go ahead, boy," Faith said. "I'll be fine. Go get him. Take Michael and find this bastard."

Turk cast a final worried look at Faith, then barked acquiescence and sprinted off with Michael after him.

Faith sighed and leaned back onto her elbows, breathing heavily. She pulled her radio out and said, "Mickel, I'm down. Turk and Michael are continuing their pursuit. I'll send you my coordinates for extraction."

"Shit, Bold," Mickel said. "Are you all right?"

"I'm all right," she said. "My ankle's sprained and possibly torn, but I'm all right. I've had this injury before. It'll heal."

"You are one tough SOB, Faith," Mickel said. "Or DOB, I guess."

Faith chuckled. "There's still some debate on that point, but I appreciate it. This will be worth it when Michael and Turk get Langeveldt."

"If they get Langeveldt," Mickel corrected.

"No," Faith insisted. "When they get Langeveldt."

116

***

Michael followed Turk for another quarter mile before the dog stopped and put his nose to the ground.

"Goddammit," Michael said softly. Louder, he said, "You got this, Turk. Just keep looking. You'll pick him up again."

Turk barked agreement and trotted a few yards ahead. Michael looked around for any sign of disturbance in the undergrowth that might indicate someone had passed this way before him. Not that he would know the difference between human sign and bear sign. He made a mental note to take the advanced survival course at Quantico as soon as he could to brush up on his wilderness skills.

Oh, dammit, bears. He completely forgot about bears.

He looked back anxiously behind him. Faith had her gun, but she wasn't mobile, and unless she got a lucky shot, it would take several nine-millimeter rounds to put down a charging bear. If a bear got to her, she might not have enough time to protect herself.

Turk barked and started off on the killer's trail. After a moment's hesitation, Michael decided to trust Faith. She was strong. She had overcome worse than this.

Even at that thought, memories of Faith in the hospital after Trammell's attack, covered in bandages and unable to walk, flooded his mind. Jethro was a seven-foot-tall three-hundred-pound giant and, as strong as Langeveldt might be, he was no Jethro Trammell.

But Faith was already injured, and Langeveldt was desperate. He wouldn't be looking to subdue Faith. He would be looking to eliminate her.

He took a deep breath and forced these worries aside. He had to trust Faith. He had to believe that she knew what she was doing.

And Turk did have a scent. That much was clear. If he and Turk caught Langeveldt, then he wouldn't be an issue anymore.

Unless this was another false scent. Turk was a good dog and an excellent K9, but he was only a dog. He could be fooled. Michael had seen that several times before now.

Still, he didn't have a choice. He certainly didn't have a lead. He could only hope that this time, Turk's confidence wasn't misplaced.

Fifteen minutes later, his faith was rewarded. Turk's cries changed and a second later, Michael could see why. He stood in front of a shallow depression in the earth, hollowed out to form a small cave

117

buttressed by the root system of the nearby trees. Michael couldn't see inside the cave, but he could hear frantic movements within.

He drew his weapon and said, "Langeveldt! We have you surrounded!" Not technically true, but what Langeveldt didn't know wouldn't hurt them. "Come out with your hands up! Come quietly if you value your life!"

That was more bluster. Michael wasn't going to start shooting unless Langeveldt gave him a reason to. Still, the more he could frighten Langeveldt, the more likely he would surrender himself.

Michael pulled his light from his belt and clicked it on. The light illuminated the first few yards of a cave that proved to be much larger than it seemed at first. Michael started inside, telling Turk to wait at the entrance in case Langeveldt got past him.

That turned out to be a smart precaution, because no sooner had he stepped inside the cave, then Langeveldt rushed him. Before Michael could react, he chopped down hard on Michael's hands. Michael dropped his gun and light and Langeveldt kicked it away.

Michael swung at Langeveldt's gut, but Langeveldt had the jump on him and sidestepped the blow before sending one of his own crashing into Michael's temple. Michael saw the blow and managed to roll with the punch but it still pushed him off his feet. He landed heavily on the floor of the cave and Langeveldt sprinted outside.

Straight into the waiting jaws of a very pissed-off German Shepherd. Langeveldt shrieked and fell forward, Turk locked onto his ankle.

"Good!" Michael called, scrambling to his feet. "Hold him!"

Turk held to the ankle, but Langeveldt wasn't finished. He lifted the leg Turk held and drove the opposite boot into Turk's stomach. The K9's jaws shredded their way down Langeveldt's leg, ripping off his boot as the dog sailed backwards into the cave.

A rush of anger coursed through Michael. He thought grimly that Langeveldt was lucky that Turk got to his feet, clearly unharmed by the blow.

"Congratulations," he called to Langeveldt, who struggled to his feet as Michael approached. "My dog's fine. So you get to live to see your day in court."

Langeveldt glared and rushed Michael again. This time, though, Michael saw him coming. He planted his feet and planted his fist on the side of Langeveldt's jaw. The blow landed solidly, but adrenaline must have lent Langeveldt superhuman strength because he kept coming, dragging Michael to the ground.

He lifted his hand to try to strike Michael, but Turk hit him and knocked him off the agent. Langeveldt cried out and Michael scrambled to his feet.

Just in time to see Langeveldt's fingers close around his gun. His eyes widened as Langeveldt grinned crazily and brought the weapon to bear on Turk.

Instinct took over. Michael threw himself forward and pushed the barrel of the gun upward so the round buried itself in the dirt.

Langeveldt glared at Michael just in time to have his lips split by Michael's fist. He cried out, and his cry was cut short by another blow.

Michael landed several more blows, only stopping when he saw Langeveldt's eyes glaze over and felt his body go limp underneath him. Turk released his ankle and backed away a few steps, glaring at Langeveldt's prone form.

Michael stood, breathing heavily, his temple sore from where Langeveldt had hit him earlier. Langeveldt breathed heavily, and his eyes blinked as he came to.

He remained still, the fight gone from him.

"Yeah, you better stay there," Michael growled. "You have the right to keep your mouth shut, asshole, and I suggest you take it."

"Michael!" Faith's voice called.

Michael looked out of the cave to see Faith approaching. Detective James supported her as she favored her right ankle, but the fact that she was on her feet at all was an encouraging sign.

Michael lifted a hand in greeting. "Hi, Faith," he said. "I brought you a present."

Faith grinned down at the supine Langeveldt. "Aww, for me? You shouldn't have."

Langeveldt closed his eyes and whimpered. If Michael hadn't seen the inside of Langeveldt's house, he would have laughed.

CHAPTER NINETEEN

Faith walked into the interrogation room where Langeveldt sat, hands and ankles bound. The killer stared ahead stonily, his face expressionless, his eyes hard. Faith lowered herself gingerly into the chair across from him. To her left, Michael stood with his arms crossed. To her right, Turk stood, tail switching back and forth as he met Langeveldt's stony expression with his own.

"Hello, Kenny," Faith said.

Langeveldt smiled softly and met her eyes. "Hello, Faith," he said impudently. "How's the ankle?"

"The ankle's fine, thank you," Faith said. "It's sprained, but nothing's torn. I'll need a brace for three weeks and some ibuprofen, but I'll be right as rain in no time."

Langeveldt shrugged. "Oh well. All one can do is try."

"You didn't do anything, asshole," Michael said. "She tripped."

Langeveldt lifted his hands, or rather his fingers since his wrists were bound to the arms of his chair. "Potato, potahto," he said. "Either way, you'll understand if I don't offer my congratulations at your good fortune, Special Agent."

Faith leaned forward and steepled her fingers. Langeveldt regarded her steadily, with a slightly contemptuous look on his face. This was a far different Langeveldt from the whimpering, mumbling, confused man they'd arrested.

"I have to say, Kenny," Faith said. "You seem much calmer than you did earlier."

"Well," he said, "I've had time to recover from the beating your partner gave me. It's unfortunate that he had his dog with him. He's a tough son of a bitch, but he's not much of a fighter. I could have taken him."

Michael chuckled and Faith said, "I don't think that's it, Kenny. You're not just more focused. You're different. Am I speaking to Kenny Langeveldt?"

Langeveldt laughed at that for a few seconds. When his laughter subsided, he said, "Oh yes. You're talking to me. That sniveling little boy is gone. He was useful to maintain my cover because he could

120

actually make himself believe that my victims were his family, but--" he lifted his fingers again "—that ship has sailed. I got rid of him on the ride over here."

Faith and Michael shared a look.

"Don't look so surprised," Langeveldt said. "I kept surrogates for my family and threw them away like garbage when they died. You couldn't possibly have believed I was sane."

Faith leaned back and regarded Langeveldt. He met her gaze and other than the flat expression in his eyes, he looked almost normal, especially compared to the other serial killers she'd interacted with. "I don't think you're insane, Langeveldt," she said. "I think you're angry."

He scoffed. "Well, I can hardly be happy tied to a chair in a police station with a veritable mountain of evidence proving my guilt. There's a solid chance that I'll avoid the death penalty by virtue of insanity, but a life in a sanitarium doesn't promise much in the way of joy."

"How terrible for you," Michael said contemptuously.

"Oh, I'm not complaining," Langeveldt said. "I knew this was coming. I let go of my fear years ago. Or rather, I gave it to the worm."

"The worm?"

"That's the name I gave my simple-minded half. He called me the lizard because I never showed any emotion when I had to handle the problems the worm would create for me."

"So you had a separate personality?"

Langeveldt cocked his head. "I wouldn't say my personality split, per se. I was always aware of the truth; I often chose not to abide by it lest I find myself at the mercy of the law earlier than necessary. I always knew this was how it ended, though. You can only get away with a life like mine for so long."

"So why?" Faith asked. "Why, if you knew how this was going to end, did you allow yourself to follow this path?"

"Like I said," Langeveldt replied, "I'm not sane. I thought I was, for a long time, but I wasn't. I thought I had put the past behind me, but it remained there, lurking in the dark, just waiting for something to tear down the thin walls I had put up and break free."

"I was not loved as a child, Special Agent. I believe my parents intended only to have two children. I was six years younger than my brother and nine years younger than my sister. I was, as polite people say, an unplanned pregnancy."

"My parents despised me. My father stonewalled me. I would be lucky to get the time of day from him. All praise, all encouragement, all pride was saved for my brother. My mother made sure to tell me explicitly how worthless and useless I was, and how I should be grateful they didn't, as she put it, toss me into a dumpster with the rest of the garbage."

Faith's eyes widened, and Langeveldt grinned. "That makes a little more sense now, doesn't it?"

He took a breath and said, "Alyssa wasn't so bad. She was as bratty and bitchy as any young woman would be to her younger brother. Still, she seemed to take particular delight in my lack of success with girls as a youth. I recall, after my brother seduced my girlfriend, she used to speculate that my manhood must be particularly small if a fourteen-year-old wouldn't even touch it."

"My brother, however. He was the worst. My parents despised me, and my sister delighted in my misfortune, but my brother was cruel. He told me often how he might inject me with an overdose of heroin and watch me choke on my own vomit."

Faith's eyes widened further and Langeveldt offered another grin. "Yes, it all comes together when you hear the whole tale. Don't look at me like that, Special Agent, I'm not making any excuses. There are healthier ways to handle a shitty family life than the outlet I chose. Still, insane as I am, I don't believe anyone could honestly tell me that there exists a more satisfying way."

"You found my fire starting implements, yes?"

Faith nodded and Langeveldt grinned. "Well, then you know of my affinity with fire. I have to tell you, Special Agent, giving up fire was the hardest part of the life I lived after my family's death. I did it, because to do otherwise was to invite disaster, but it was hard. Even when I believed I was well-adjusted, I would spend hours staring at my fireplace and wishing to God I was seeing again the inferno that claimed my family."

"But I didn't give in. Even when I saw the image of my brother kissing my former girlfriend, the one he stole from me, I never used fire as a method of murder."

He cocked his head again and said, "In hindsight, she probably wasn't Angie. She was most likely wearing earrings and from a distance the gleam looked to me like the little birthmark I found so fascinating as a youth. Well, anyway, it doesn't matter. I never hurt her."

"But you hurt the man you thought looked like your brother."

"Oh yes. I've killed seventeen people, Special Agent, not including my family."

Faith expected the number to be higher than the three they knew of, but hearing the actual count still drove a stake through her heart.

Langeveldt smiled, and for a brief instant, Faith thought she detected a hint of regret in that smile. "Like I said, Special Agent. I'm not sane."

"Yeah, you hold onto that," Michael interjected. "Maybe you'll get lucky and find a jury that actually believes it."

"It doesn't matter," Langeveldt said. "They'll believe in the story even if they don't believe me. People are fascinated with killers like me, Special Agent. As long as people like me are safely put away, they like knowing that we're out there somewhere. They like reading about a tragedy and wondering for a moment if their pet slasher is responsible."

Faith wasn't in the mood to hear Langeveldt's judgement of humanity, but she was curious about one thing.

"Why did you drug them, Kenny? Why, instead of burning them, did you drug them instead?"

"I already told you why I didn't use fire a second time," Langeveldt said. "As for why I drugged them?"

His contemptuous smile faded, replaced by the flat, expressionless look he wore when Faith came in. His voice was as flat as his expression when he spoke next, and Faith could understand why the other half of Langeveldt's psyche would refer to this half as the lizard.

"I was powerless as a child, Special Agent. Powerless. I was six years younger than my brother. I never even approached him in strength. Not while he was alive, anyway. Even my sister could overpower me. She sometimes did. Can you imagine, Special Agent, how much it damages a young person's psyche to be held down physically and forced to remain still while your brother did unspeakable things to you? Can you imagine how much it damages a psyche when it is a young boy being held down by his sister?"

"Are you saying you were molested by your brother?"

"Oh no, nothing like that. My brother peed on me once when he was eleven and I was five. No doubt he forgot the incident a week after it happened, but I never did. I could share hundreds of stories with you, Special Agent, but they all boil down to me being utterly powerless and my brother and sister being utterly cruel in the face of that powerlessness, while my parents tacitly encouraged the behavior."

"I'm not powerless anymore."

He glanced down at his bonds and said, "Well, *now* I am. But I wasn't. For a long time, I wasn't. And I *so* enjoyed making them powerless!"

He grinned with evil as he said that, and for the first time, Faith believed that he actually was insane. Maybe not so insane as to justify his behavior in any way, but clearly unwell.

"My brother and sister had no choice but to sit and stare, unable to move while I did whatever I wanted to them." His grin took on an air of sickening pride, and he said, "And I used it to treat them kindly. I made them homemade meals and talked to them. I put on tv shows for them; I bathed them. Did you know that? Probably you did. You saw them. You could tell that someone must have wiped their respective asses for them."

Faith's lips curled in contempt, and Langeveldt said, "You have to give me some credit for that. How many murderers do you know are so kind to their victims?"

When Faith didn't respond, Langeveldt sighed and continued. "Anyway, I found that the power was enough to satisfy me. I didn't need to torture them. I didn't need to burn them or cut them. I didn't need to violate them. I just needed to talk to them. I needed someone to listen. With my desire for revenge satisfied, I needed to experience, even in the smallest sense, what it feels like to have a loving, supportive family."

"So, I created a world where that family existed. I gave them personalities that, while similar to their actual personalities, weren't so cruel. Dad became a gruff curmudgeon instead of cold and loveless. Mom became a gossip and a busybody instead of ruthlessly judgmental. Alyssa became a bimbo instead of a bitch, and my brother became an annoying but lovable alpha instead of a sadistic jerk. It was a family I could accept and most importantly, a family that accepted me."

"I realize how foolish this all is, Special Agent. I understand how ridiculous it is of me to engage in this farce. I know that those men and women were innocents whose lives I ended terribly. I know that my family died never loving me, in fact, probably confirmed in their hatred for me. I know that I've gained no revenge by taking my anger out on others. I'm not defending myself. But all I have to do for the rest of my life, however long that is, is talk, and so I have."

"You burned them," Michael said. "I don't understand. You killed your family. You already got revenge. You even got away with it. You won. Why did you need to kill other people?"

Langeveldt took a breath. "I didn't win, Special Agent. I'll never win. One of my earliest memories is my sister holding me still while my brother pissed on me. You don't overcome a start like that. I tried. I really did. I tried hard, but it only took one look at a couple who reminded me of my brother and my first love for me to break completely."

"I won't insult your intelligence by asking you to feel sorry for me, but I do feel sorry for myself. If I could have had a normal upbringing, who knows what I could have been? I'm smart. I'm a good problem-solver. I'm calm under pressure. I could have been successful in anything I chose to do."

"And that's just it, Kenny," Faith said. "You *chose* to be a serial killer. You *chose* to kill your family. You *chose* to give in to your trauma. I've been where you are now, Kenny. I understand what it's like to feel powerless, and I understand what it's like to feel trapped by your past."

"I understand what it's like to be obsessed with revenge."

She paused a moment. Langeveldt regarded her with his flat expression. "I understand what it's like to believe that there's no way out. But there is. You have to choose to stay on that path, and you have to choose to remain there no matter what comes into your life to try to pull you off of it. You didn't choose to stay on your path, and because you chose to stray, seventeen innocent people have lost their lives."

"So have I," Langeveldt said, his expression unchanged.

Faith nodded and stood. She wasn't sure exactly why she had wasted her time telling Langeveldt that. Maybe she simply needed to hear it herself. She hadn't gone off the deep end the way Langeveldt had, but she really did understand the feeling of being a slave to her past.

Still, she felt no sympathy for Langeveldt. Langeveldt viewed other lives as meaningless compared to his own, and Faith didn't believe that any amount of trauma justified that belief.

She walked toward the door, Michael and Turk following.

"Thank you for listening," Langeveldt called after her.

She didn't respond.

CHAPTER TWENTY

"Do I get to sign the cast?" Michael asked.

Faith rolled her eyes. "There's no cast, Michael, but if you want to sign my Ace bandage, you can feel free."

Michael chuckled and pulled out a sharpie. "I'm going to write, 'Michael was here.'"

Faith waited until Michael was on his knees, then smiled sweetly and said, "You were."

Michael looked up at her uncertainly for a moment, and she laughed. He rolled his eyes and got back to his seat. "You know what? Forget it. I'm going to leave my past behind too."

"Aww, does that mean you miss me?" Faith teased.

"I miss when you were easy to deal with," Michael groused.

"Well, you never quite figured that part out," Faith said, "but on a serious note, I miss being your friend. I've been talking to Doctor West, and... he's right. I've been obsessing over the copycat case so much that it's affected my relationships, especially my relationship with you. I'm sorry about that. I hate thinking that my inability to overcome my past could be destroying my future and hurting people I care about."

"Yeah," Michael said, "I gotta tell you, Faith, for being so smart, you're the biggest idiot I've ever known."

"Ouch," Faith replied. "I deserved that."

"Yeah, but not for the reason you think."

Michael locked eyes with Faith and said, "You were always my friend, Faith. Always. That's never changed. I was pissed at you, and things were awkward, but it's only the third time things have been awkward between us in ten years. You're my friend, and more importantly, you're my partner. I love you. Not in the romantic sense, so don't get all stupid, but I love you. You're my best friend, and I'm not going to toss you aside just because you're jealous of my new girlfriend."

Faith's smile faded, and she lowered her eyes.

"Hey, I was just teasing, Faith," Michael said. "I didn't mean—"

"No, it's not that," Faith said. "I... David and I are taking a break."

"Oh," Michael said. "Oh, I'm sorry."

"It's all right," Faith shrugged, managing to regain her smile. "I don't think this is the end. Just a bit of breathing room for both of us. To be honest, I kind of need a break too. I have some stuff to work on. We'll be okay."

Michael offered a comforting hand and Faith took it. He squeezed it briefly, then said, "Anything I can do to help? I know some guys in prison who can knock him around a bit if—"

Faith pulled her hand away, rolling her eyes as Michael laughed. "It's moments like these that remind me exactly why I am *not* jealous of Ellie."

"Well," Michael said, "that's debatable, but the part about friendship is true. You're my friend, and you're always going to be my friend. Just don't be so grouchy when people don't agree with everything you say right away."

"I'm not grouchy when—"

"Oh yes you are," Michael interrupted. "Ten years, remember? I've slept next to you more than I've slept next to my girlfriend since I met her, and I am *not* proud of that fact."

"Well, you're not always a joy to be around either," Faith retorted. She screwed her face up in a frown and mimicked Michael. "Oh, it's so terrible. My lead didn't pan out. It's taking too damn long. It's too hot."

"All right," Michael said, rolling his eyes, "You've made your point."

"Coffee sucks!" Faith said, still in Michael's voice. "I hate this coffee! Why don't they have any good coffee? Where's the coffee?"

"You know, you're a dick to men who are vulnerable with you," Michael said, "and that's the real reason David needs a break."

"Coffee!" Faith growled.

Michael couldn't hold back anymore. He burst into laughter, throwing his head back and making enough noise that several people turned to look at them.

Faith joined him, and for a moment, her grief washed completely away.

***

"I'm so sorry," Doctor West said gently.

Faith took a deep breath. "Yeah. Me too."

"Are you okay?"

Faith chuckled. "You're my doctor. You tell me."

127

Doctor West considered a moment, then shook his head. "No. You are most definitely not okay."

"No," Faith chuckled. "I am not."

They laughed together a moment, then Doctor West said, "I'm proud of you."

Faith nodded. "Yeah. Me too."

"I heard you reconciled with Michael, though. That's good."

"Yes," Faith said, "it is good. I missed him a lot more than I thought I would."

"We rarely understand how valuable our loved ones all until we've nearly lost them."

"Yeah," Faith said, "It's a bitch."

Doctor West chuckled. "It is. A raging bitch. But you've taken the right steps to keep them. You've admitted your own fears and you've accepted theirs. You've heard them out, and you've agreed to do your part to mend the bridges between you. Michael's already come around. David will too."

"You think so?" Faith asked.

"Oh yes. He needs time to see you're serious. Michael has the advantage in that he's known you for ten years. He knows that once you're pushed to the point where you finally admit your fears and doubts, you'll leave them behind and conquer whatever hill it is you have to climb. David's not there yet, but this will show him."

Faith narrowed her eyes. "You know, I don't know how I feel about being analyzed like this."

"It annoys you immensely, but strangely comforts you to know that someone understands your motivations and still doesn't judge you for them."

"Is telling me my own thoughts gonna be a thing?" Faith asked playfully. "Because if it is, I want a new therapist."

"Well, good luck convincing your boss of that," Doctor West said. "He's pissed at you enough to plant you on a desk at the first sign of trouble."

"Oh, I think I can get him to come around," Faith said.

"How's that?"

"I'm going to apologize for my interference in the copycat Donkey Killer case, and I'm going to leave it in my past."

Doctor West stared blankly at her. Faith grinned at the obvious shock the news had caused him. "Oh?" he finally said.

128

She nodded. "I haven't told you about the D.C. case yet, but long story short, our killer went completely off the deep end because of some trauma in his past. Obviously, I'm not going to murder dozens of people, but I was close to ruining my life because of bad memories. I'm not going to do that anymore. I won't let Jethro Trammell rule me. I'm leaving him behind, and I'm leaving the case behind."

She expected an explosion of encouragement, but Doctor West was apparently still too surprised to react. Finally, he managed a smile and said, "That's incredible, Faith! Congratulations!"

Faith grinned and said, "Thank you."

Doctor West smiled. "You're welcome."

"No," Faith said, "I mean it. Thank you. I didn't want a therapist. Like you said, it annoyed me, but it means a lot to have someone to hear the worst of my life and guide me out of it. You've helped me overcome my greatest demon, and I can't tell you how much it means to me."

Doctor West flushed and looked away, and Faith thought he looked adorable. He straightened his tie, coughed, and said, "Well, yes. Thank you. I mean, I'm glad."

Faith laughed and joked, "You're cute when you blush."

Doctor West smiled but didn't offer a rebuttal.

***

"Hey, Faith!" Clark said, grinning. "Come on in! Do you want a drink? The boss knows about the bottle, so you're in the clear if you want to try some."

Faith shook her head. "No thank you, Clark. I just... I need to tell you something."

"Oh, don't worry about it," Clark said. "I know you resented me for being your supervisor, and I don't blame you. It's kinda like when Kobe had to take orders from Byron Scott, and just decided to torpedo his own career instead." His smile disappeared. "Gosh, that was a terrible reference. I'm sorry about that. I only meant that you're one of the greatest agents of all time, so it must hurt to have a grunt giving you orders."

Faith smiled. "I wouldn't have understood the reference anyway. I'm more of a hockey girl myself."

129

"Ah. Well, I don't know jack about hockey, so you'll have to look up Byron Scott. I'm sure you know who Kobe is. Please tell me you know who Kobe is."

"I know," Faith said, "and I won't lie. It does chafe a little that I'm basically on probation right now, but that's not what I have to tell you."

Clark nodded. "You thought I was the guy."

Faith blinked. "What?"

"You thought I was the copycat. The new Trammell."

Faith stared at him in shock. Absurdly, her first thought was that Clark was a much better detective than she gave him credit for.

Clark nodded. "Yeah, I thought for a moment that you might think that. I didn't believe it until now, but it did cross my mind briefly. Faith, can I tell you something?"

Faith nodded. "Of course."

Clark met her gaze and said seriously, "You have the potential to be the greatest Special Agent in FBI history. But you need to let go of your obsession with the copycat killer case. You don't think clearly when you obsess about something. Obsession is never about the truth. It's about *your* truth. It's about what you want to believe. You will ignore every fact and twist others that aren't even there to justify your decision to remain obsessed. I've been obsessed before. I've lost my entire life before."

Faith didn't let on that she already knew the details of Clark's past. She only listened as he said, "I don't want that for you. You're better than anyone at this job. You're better than me."

"I'm not so sure about that anymore," Faith said and meant it.

"I am," Clark said. "So please don't throw it away over some punk hillbilly who liked to cut people."

Faith smiled and said, "Well, you're right. I have let it go. I'm going to leave it behind."

"That's good," Clark said, "that's good. You gotta tell yourself that every day. I didn't. That's why I went after the Juarez family anyway."

Faith blinked in shock again.

Clark smiled. "The boss gave me access to your Bureau email and cellphone records. I intercepted your messages to Abel."

Faith reddened and Clark said, "It's all right. If I thought you were a serial killer, I'd look you up too. Next time, though, get a burner phone and mail him one from any address that isn't your home address. If you're careful about it, the Bureau will never find out."

"Good to know," Faith said, "and I'm sorry. And thank you."

"Don't mention it," Clark said. "I won't tell Abel. He's a good SAC. If he transitions to information management, then he'll be a good section chief one day. Besides," he shrugged. "It's nice to have someone besides me know what happened. Just don't tell anyone, please. Not even Michael. Prince is a good guy, but I'd rather this stayed between us."

"It will," Faith promised. "Thank you again... Boss."

Clark beamed at her and said cheerfully, "If you ever call me boss again, I will personally throw you out of the Bureau myself."

Faith laughed and said, "Fair enough." She stood. "I'll catch you later, Clark."

"See you later, Faith."

She stepped outside and met Turk in the break room. He wagged his tail and jumped up to greet her. She endured ten seconds or so of face-licking before Turk finally dropped down.

"Good to see you too, boy," she said. "Let's go home."

EPILOGUE

How dare she? How dare she forget about him like he was nothing? Like he meant nothing? He may not be the architect, but he was at the very least the architect's master student if he hadn't already exceeded him. How could she, the unfinished masterpiece, scorn him?

Well, no matter. She might think she had overcome her past, but she hadn't. Her mind was still fragile. Not as fragile as it was a few months ago, and that was a mistake, but she was still fragile. A little push in the right direction, and she would be his again.

And he knew just where to push.

It was one thing to lose the memory of one's greatest trauma, but what about the hope of one's salvation? If she lost that, if he *took* it from her, there would be no recovery. There would be no leaving behind. She would be his again, as was only right, as was only *just.*

He entered the café and stood in line. David stood five people ahead of him, his face drawn and his eyes blocked by heavy sunglasses. He was grieving the loss of his relationship just as Faith was. That drivel about David taking her back was just that—drivel—but it served his purposes to allow Faith hope.

And now it served his purposes to take away that hope. She needed to have nothing in her life that could distract her from him. The other agent, Prince, would have been a better choice, but he was untouchable. He wasn't nearly so clever as Faith, but he was aware of his own surroundings. He couldn't conceive of a way to overcome him.

But the vet, he could handle. He was a civilian, and as defenseless as any other civilian in the mightiest, wealthiest nation on Earth. He had no need to concern himself with his own safety. He had police for that.

He could take the vet.

David placed his order and stepped to the side to wait for his latte. He caught the man's gaze and nodded perfunctorily. The man smiled and nodded more genially, then looked ahead and placed his own order. A moment later, David left the coffee shop and drove to work. The man never turned his head.

132

NOW AVAILABLE!

SO LOST
(A Faith Bold Mystery—Book 6)

FBI Special Agent Faith Bold needs her K9 German Shepherd, Turk, to help her when victims of a new serial killer are found buried alive in graveyards, a mysterious string tied around their finger. Only Faith and Turk can save the next victim before her time runs out—but this killer is always one step ahead and they may have finally met their match….

"A masterpiece of thriller and mystery."
—Books and Movie Reviews, Roberto Mattos (re Once Gone)

SO LOST is Book #6 in a long-anticipated new series by #1 bestseller and USA Today bestselling author Blake Pierce, whose bestseller Once Gone (a free download) has received over 7,000 five star ratings and reviews.

FBI Special Agent Faith Bold doesn't believe she can ever return to the force after the trauma she's been through. Suffering from past demons, she feels unfit for duty and content to retire—until Turk walks into her life.

Turk, a former Marine Corps dog, wounded in battle, suffers from his own demons. But he never lets it show as he gives everything to Faith to get her back on her feet.

Each are slow to warm up to each other, but when they do, they are inseparable. Each is equally determined to hunt down the demons chasing them, whatever the cost, and to watch each other's backs—even at the risk of their own life.

A page-turning and harrowing crime thriller featuring a brilliant and tortured FBI agent, the Faith Bold series is a riveting mystery, packed with non-stop action, suspense, twists and turns, revelations, and driven by a breakneck pace that will keep you flipping pages late into the night. Fans of Rachel Caine, Teresa Driscoll and Robert Dugoni are sure to fall in love.

Future books in the series are now also available.

"An edge of your seat thriller in a new series that keeps you turning pages! ...So many twists, turns and red herrings... I can't wait to see what happens next."
—Reader review (Her Last Wish)

"A strong, complex story about two FBI agents trying to stop a serial killer. If you want an author to capture your attention and have you guessing, yet trying to put the pieces together, Pierce is your author!"
—Reader review (Her Last Wish)

"A typical Blake Pierce twisting, turning, roller coaster ride suspense thriller. Will have you turning the pages to the last sentence of the last chapter!!!"
—Reader review (City of Prey)

"Right from the start we have an unusual protagonist that I haven't seen done in this genre before. The action is nonstop... A very atmospheric novel that will keep you turning pages well into the wee hours."
—Reader review (City of Prey)

"Everything that I look for in a book... a great plot, interesting characters, and grabs your interest right away. The book moves along at a breakneck pace and stays that way until the end. Now on go I to book two!"
—Reader review (Girl, Alone)

"Exciting, heart pounding, edge of your seat book... a must read for mystery and suspense readers!"
—Reader review (Girl, Alone)

Blake Pierce

Blake Pierce is the USA Today bestselling author of the RILEY PAGE mystery series, which includes seventeen books. Blake Pierce is also the author of the MACKENZIE WHITE mystery series, comprising fourteen books; of the AVERY BLACK mystery series, comprising six books; of the KERI LOCKE mystery series, comprising five books; of the MAKING OF RILEY PAIGE mystery series, comprising six books; of the KATE WISE mystery series, comprising seven books; of the CHLOE FINE psychological suspense mystery, comprising six books; of the JESSIE HUNT psychological suspense thriller series, comprising twenty-eight books; of the AU PAIR psychological suspense thriller series, comprising three books; of the ZOE PRIME mystery series, comprising six books; of the ADELE SHARP mystery series, comprising sixteen books, of the EUROPEAN VOYAGE cozy mystery series, comprising six books; of the LAURA FROST FBI suspense thriller, comprising eleven books; of the ELLA DARK FBI suspense thriller, comprising fourteen books (and counting); of the A YEAR IN EUROPE cozy mystery series, comprising nine books, of the AVA GOLD mystery series, comprising six books; of the RACHEL GIFT mystery series, comprising ten books (and counting); of the VALERIE LAW mystery series, comprising nine books (and counting); of the PAIGE KING mystery series, comprising eight books (and counting); of the MAY MOORE mystery series, comprising eleven books; of the CORA SHIELDS mystery series, comprising eight books (and counting); of the NICKY LYONS mystery series, comprising eight books (and counting), of the CAMI LARK mystery series, comprising eight books (and counting), of the AMBER YOUNG mystery series, comprising five books (and counting), of the DAISY FORTUNE mystery series, comprising five books (and counting), of the FIONA RED mystery series, comprising five books (and counting), of the FAITH BOLD mystery series, comprising eight books (and counting), of the JULIETTE HART mystery series, comprising five books (and counting), of the MORGAN CROSS mystery series, comprising five books (and counting), and of the new FINN WRIGHT mystery series, comprising five books (and counting).

An avid reader and lifelong fan of the mystery and thriller genres,

Blake loves to hear from you, so please feel free to visit www.blakepierceauthor.com to learn more and stay in touch.

BOOKS BY BLAKE PIERCE

FINN WRIGHT MYSTERY SERIES
WHEN YOU'RE MINE (Book #1)
WHEN YOU'RE SAFE (Book #2)
WHEN YOU'RE CLOSE (Book #3)
WHEN YOU'RE SLEEPING (Book #4)
WHEN YOU'RE SANE (Book #5)

MORGAN CROSS MYSTERY SERIES
FOR YOU (Book #1)
FOR RAGE (Book #2)
FOR LUST (Book #3)
FOR WRATH (Book #4)
FOREVER (Book #5)

JULIETTE HART MYSTERY SERIES
NOTHING TO FEAR (Book #1)
NOTHING THERE (Book #2)
NOTHING WATCHING (Book #3)
NOTHING HIDING (Book #4)
NOTHING LEFT (Book #5)

FAITH BOLD MYSTERY SERIES
SO LONG (Book #1)
SO COLD (Book #2)
SO SCARED (Book #3)
SO NORMAL (Book #4)
SO FAR GONE (Book #5)
SO LOST (Book #6)
SO ALONE (Book #7)
SO FORGOTTEN (Book #8)

FIONA RED MYSTERY SERIES
LET HER GO (Book #1)
LET HER BE (Book #2)
LET HER HOPE (Book #3)

LET HER WISH (Book #4)
LET HER LIVE (Book #5)

DAISY FORTUNE MYSTERY SERIES
NEED YOU (Book #1)
CLAIM YOU (Book #2)
CRAVE YOU (Book #3)
CHOOSE YOU (Book #4)
CHASE YOU (Book #5)

AMBER YOUNG MYSTERY SERIES
ABSENT PITY (Book #1)
ABSENT REMORSE (Book #2)
ABSENT FEELING (Book #3)
ABSENT MERCY (Book #4)
ABSENT REASON (Book #5)

CAMI LARK MYSTERY SERIES
JUST ME (Book #1)
JUST OUTSIDE (Book #2)
JUST RIGHT (Book #3)
JUST FORGET (Book #4)
JUST ONCE (Book #5)
JUST HIDE (Book #6)
JUST NOW (Book #7)
JUST HOPE (Book #8)

NICKY LYONS MYSTERY SERIES
ALL MINE (Book #1)
ALL HIS (Book #2)
ALL HE SEES (Book #3)
ALL ALONE (Book #4)
ALL FOR ONE (Book #5)
ALL HE TAKES (Book #6)
ALL FOR ME (Book #7)
ALL IN (Book #8)

CORA SHIELDS MYSTERY SERIES
UNDONE (Book #1)
UNWANTED (Book #2)

UNHINGED (Book #3)
UNSAID (Book #4)
UNGLUED (Book #5)
UNSTABLE (Book #6)
UNKNOWN (Book #7)
UNAWARE (Book #8)

MAY MOORE SUSPENSE THRILLER
NEVER RUN (Book #1)
NEVER TELL (Book #2)
NEVER LIVE (Book #3)
NEVER HIDE (Book #4)
NEVER FORGIVE (Book #5)
NEVER AGAIN (Book #6)
NEVER LOOK BACK (Book #7)
NEVER FORGET (Book #8)
NEVER LET GO (Book #9)
NEVER PRETEND (Book #10)
NEVER HESITATE (Book #11)

PAIGE KING MYSTERY SERIES
THE GIRL HE PINED (Book #1)
THE GIRL HE CHOSE (Book #2)
THE GIRL HE TOOK (Book #3)
THE GIRL HE WISHED (Book #4)
THE GIRL HE CROWNED (Book #5)
THE GIRL HE WATCHED (Book #6)
THE GIRL HE WANTED (Book #7)
THE GIRL HE CLAIMED (Book #8)

VALERIE LAW MYSTERY SERIES
NO MERCY (Book #1)
NO PITY (Book #2)
NO FEAR (Book #3)
NO SLEEP (Book #4)
NO QUARTER (Book #5)
NO CHANCE (Book #6)
NO REFUGE (Book #7)
NO GRACE (Book #8)
NO ESCAPE (Book #9)

RACHEL GIFT MYSTERY SERIES
HER LAST WISH (Book #1)
HER LAST CHANCE (Book #2)
HER LAST HOPE (Book #3)
HER LAST FEAR (Book #4)
HER LAST CHOICE (Book #5)
HER LAST BREATH (Book #6)
HER LAST MISTAKE (Book #7)
HER LAST DESIRE (Book #8)
HER LAST REGRET (Book #9)
HER LAST HOUR (Book #10)

AVA GOLD MYSTERY SERIES
CITY OF PREY (Book #1)
CITY OF FEAR (Book #2)
CITY OF BONES (Book #3)
CITY OF GHOSTS (Book #4)
CITY OF DEATH (Book #5)
CITY OF VICE (Book #6)

A YEAR IN EUROPE
A MURDER IN PARIS (Book #1)
DEATH IN FLORENCE (Book #2)
VENGEANCE IN VIENNA (Book #3)
A FATALITY IN SPAIN (Book #4)

ELLA DARK FBI SUSPENSE THRILLER
GIRL, ALONE (Book #1)
GIRL, TAKEN (Book #2)
GIRL, HUNTED (Book #3)
GIRL, SILENCED (Book #4)
GIRL, VANISHED (Book 5)
GIRL ERASED (Book #6)
GIRL, FORSAKEN (Book #7)
GIRL, TRAPPED (Book #8)
GIRL, EXPENDABLE (Book #9)
GIRL, ESCAPED (Book #10)
GIRL, HIS (Book #11)
GIRL, LURED (Book #12)

GIRL, MISSING (Book #13)
GIRL, UNKNOWN (Book #14)

LAURA FROST FBI SUSPENSE THRILLER
ALREADY GONE (Book #1)
ALREADY SEEN (Book #2)
ALREADY TRAPPED (Book #3)
ALREADY MISSING (Book #4)
ALREADY DEAD (Book #5)
ALREADY TAKEN (Book #6)
ALREADY CHOSEN (Book #7)
ALREADY LOST (Book #8)
ALREADY HIS (Book #9)
ALREADY LURED (Book #10)
ALREADY COLD (Book #11)

EUROPEAN VOYAGE COZY MYSTERY SERIES
MURDER (AND BAKLAVA) (Book #1)
DEATH (AND APPLE STRUDEL) (Book #2)
CRIME (AND LAGER) (Book #3)
MISFORTUNE (AND GOUDA) (Book #4)
CALAMITY (AND A DANISH) (Book #5)
MAYHEM (AND HERRING) (Book #6)

ADELE SHARP MYSTERY SERIES
LEFT TO DIE (Book #1)
LEFT TO RUN (Book #2)
LEFT TO HIDE (Book #3)
LEFT TO KILL (Book #4)
LEFT TO MURDER (Book #5)
LEFT TO ENVY (Book #6)
LEFT TO LAPSE (Book #7)
LEFT TO VANISH (Book #8)
LEFT TO HUNT (Book #9)
LEFT TO FEAR (Book #10)
LEFT TO PREY (Book #11)
LEFT TO LURE (Book #12)
LEFT TO CRAVE (Book #13)
LEFT TO LOATHE (Book #14)
LEFT TO HARM (Book #15)

LEFT TO RUIN (Book #16)

THE AU PAIR SERIES
ALMOST GONE (Book#1)
ALMOST LOST (Book #2)
ALMOST DEAD (Book #3)

ZOE PRIME MYSTERY SERIES
FACE OF DEATH (Book#1)
FACE OF MURDER (Book #2)
FACE OF FEAR (Book #3)
FACE OF MADNESS (Book #4)
FACE OF FURY (Book #5)
FACE OF DARKNESS (Book #6)

A JESSIE HUNT PSYCHOLOGICAL SUSPENSE SERIES
THE PERFECT WIFE (Book #1)
THE PERFECT BLOCK (Book #2)
THE PERFECT HOUSE (Book #3)
THE PERFECT SMILE (Book #4)
THE PERFECT LIE (Book #5)
THE PERFECT LOOK (Book #6)
THE PERFECT AFFAIR (Book #7)
THE PERFECT ALIBI (Book #8)
THE PERFECT NEIGHBOR (Book #9)
THE PERFECT DISGUISE (Book #10)
THE PERFECT SECRET (Book #11)
THE PERFECT FAÇADE (Book #12)
THE PERFECT IMPRESSION (Book #13)
THE PERFECT DECEIT (Book #14)
THE PERFECT MISTRESS (Book #15)
THE PERFECT IMAGE (Book #16)
THE PERFECT VEIL (Book #17)
THE PERFECT INDISCRETION (Book #18)
THE PERFECT RUMOR (Book #19)
THE PERFECT COUPLE (Book #20)
THE PERFECT MURDER (Book #21)
THE PERFECT HUSBAND (Book #22)
THE PERFECT SCANDAL (Book #23)
THE PERFECT MASK (Book #24)

THE PERFECT RUSE (Book #25)
THE PERFECT VENEER (Book #26)
THE PERFECT PEOPLE (Book #27)
THE PERFECT WITNESS (Book #28)

CHLOE FINE PSYCHOLOGICAL SUSPENSE SERIES
NEXT DOOR (Book #1)
A NEIGHBOR'S LIE (Book #2)
CUL DE SAC (Book #3)
SILENT NEIGHBOR (Book #4)
HOMECOMING (Book #5)
TINTED WINDOWS (Book #6)

KATE WISE MYSTERY SERIES
IF SHE KNEW (Book #1)
IF SHE SAW (Book #2)
IF SHE RAN (Book #3)
IF SHE HID (Book #4)
IF SHE FLED (Book #5)
IF SHE FEARED (Book #6)
IF SHE HEARD (Book #7)

THE MAKING OF RILEY PAIGE SERIES
WATCHING (Book #1)
WAITING (Book #2)
LURING (Book #3)
TAKING (Book #4)
STALKING (Book #5)
KILLING (Book #6)

RILEY PAIGE MYSTERY SERIES
ONCE GONE (Book #1)
ONCE TAKEN (Book #2)
ONCE CRAVED (Book #3)
ONCE LURED (Book #4)
ONCE HUNTED (Book #5)
ONCE PINED (Book #6)
ONCE FORSAKEN (Book #7)
ONCE COLD (Book #8)
ONCE STALKED (Book #9)

ONCE LOST (Book #10)
ONCE BURIED (Book #11)
ONCE BOUND (Book #12)
ONCE TRAPPED (Book #13)
ONCE DORMANT (Book #14)
ONCE SHUNNED (Book #15)
ONCE MISSED (Book #16)
ONCE CHOSEN (Book #17)

MACKENZIE WHITE MYSTERY SERIES
BEFORE HE KILLS (Book #1)
BEFORE HE SEES (Book #2)
BEFORE HE COVETS (Book #3)
BEFORE HE TAKES (Book #4)
BEFORE HE NEEDS (Book #5)
BEFORE HE FEELS (Book #6)
BEFORE HE SINS (Book #7)
BEFORE HE HUNTS (Book #8)
BEFORE HE PREYS (Book #9)
BEFORE HE LONGS (Book #10)
BEFORE HE LAPSES (Book #11)
BEFORE HE ENVIES (Book #12)
BEFORE HE STALKS (Book #13)
BEFORE HE HARMS (Book #14)

AVERY BLACK MYSTERY SERIES
CAUSE TO KILL (Book #1)
CAUSE TO RUN (Book #2)
CAUSE TO HIDE (Book #3)
CAUSE TO FEAR (Book #4)
CAUSE TO SAVE (Book #5)
CAUSE TO DREAD (Book #6)

KERI LOCKE MYSTERY SERIES
A TRACE OF DEATH (Book #1)
A TRACE OF MURDER (Book #2)
A TRACE OF VICE (Book #3)
A TRACE OF CRIME (Book #4)
A TRACE OF HOPE (Book #5)

Made in the USA
Middletown, DE
06 September 2023

38066521R00092